Was There Ever
Seen
Such Villainy?

Peter Carpmael

Trafford
PUBLISHING™

 www.trafford.com

North America & international
toll-free: 1 888 232 4444 (USA & Canada)
phone: 250 383 6864 ♦ fax: 250 383 6804 ♦ email: info@trafford.com

The United Kingdom & Europe
phone: +44 (0)1865 722 113 ♦ local rate: 0845 230 9601
facsimile: +44 (0)1865 722 868 ♦ email: info.uk@trafford.com

10 9 8 7 6 5 4 3

For my darling wife, Tot

and our three sons: Patrick, John and James

Acknowledgements

I want to acknowledge the assistance of all my family in preparing this novel for publication, and also the technical support in the preparation of the cover picture given by Cameron Toms.

The portrait, which is thought to be of Christopher Marlowe, is reproduced by kind permission of The Master and Fellows of Corpus Christi College, Cambridge.

Contents

*"Why, was there ever seen such villainy, so neatly
plotted..."*

- *The Jew of Malta* - Christopher Marlowe (1564 – 1593)

Cornwall

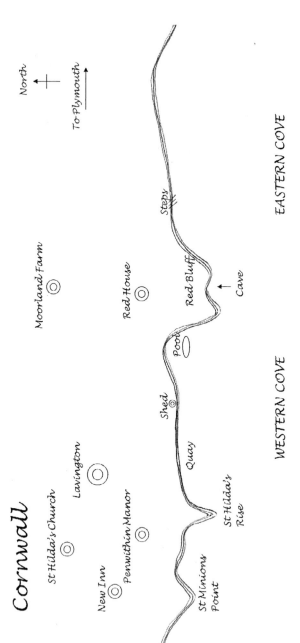

North

To Plymouth

St Hilda's Church

Lavington

New Inn

Penwithin Manor

Moorland Farm

St Minions Point

St Hilda's Rise

Quay

Shed

Red House

Pool

Red Bluff

Cave

Steps

WESTERN COVE

EASTERN COVE

Was There Ever Seen Such Villainy?

Part 1:

The Cave: 23rd September, 1946

"…I will live; nor loathe I this my life:
And, since you leave me in the ocean thus
To sink or swim, and put me to my shifts,
I'll rouse my senses, and awake myself."

- *The Jew of Malta* - Christopher Marlowe

I

The blood red sun dips steadily below the western skyline in a multi-coloured spectacle, quickly replacing the dissolving crimson line with the blanket of night. Much later the moon rises transforming the desert into a pale landscape, eerie as the surface of the moon.

"Will they come tonight, sir?" the sergeant asks.

"We'll know soon enough," Harry Guest replies.

Not put off, the N.C.O. persists, "Are we on mine-laying again tomorrow, sir?"

"No. After three weeks non-stop, I think we'll stay where we are until they come."

Harry walks on to the next slit trench as part of his regular checks of the platoon's forward positions. Each night the sentry wakens him for his turn on duty, shaking his shoulder and every time, automatically, his right hand drops to the butt of his service revolver in its webbing holster – a self-protective reflex. Then, he is on his feet, staring round at the moonscape wilderness.

"Will they come tonight?"

Looking to the South, as if some comfort lies in that empty region, he shakes his head. Well known fact, the Quattara Depression denies the way to all transport, tracked or otherwise. Only specially equipped troops such as the Long Range Desert Group can operate across the soft sands which cover the whole area. Behind him stretches the Mediterranean; and the El Alamein line lies between the sea in the North and the sand sea here in the South.

Instinctively turning sharply to face the West, he becomes aware of a change in the atmosphere. Then the sky is suddenly lit up. Flares streak into the night along the horizon accompanied by a series of explosions. The flares open out, following one another as they drift illuminating a vast pattern of desert for the advancing enemy. The mobile glare flickers from spluttering flares, each suspended on individual parachutes swinging erratically. In addition the flashing gunfire from massed artillery disturbs the night like continuous summer lightning.

"They're coming."

At this moment of theatrical crescendo Harry wavers. The moving lights seem to affect his surroundings. And, gradually, he is overwhelmed by a feeling of dizziness as if the world about him is turning slowly. Simultaneously the explosions fade; the desert becomes silent; and he is watching the approaching enemy attack as though it was taking place in a film which has lost the sound track. And then a shutter snaps down cutting off his vision; and he blacks out altogether.

When he opens his eyes, he closes them at once, afraid of unknown surroundings. The desert has vanished altogether. The noise of war has gone.

"Where am I? What is happening?"

As he slowly revives from deep unconsciousness, he becomes aware of the beginning of fear. "Can I move?" Cautiously he stretches stiff limbs and opens his eyes again, wide.

Reality. He is inside a large cave and lying on a ledge of wet rock. As he lifts his head, he feels an acute stab of pain. He lets his fingers gently explore and discover a long wound at the back of his head, where the skin has been torn open under the hair. As he touches the congealed scar, it immediately starts to bleed.

Harry remains still. He is a tall, heavily built young man, dark-haired with dense black eyebrows and dark brown eyes. His small military moustache adds an air of authority to his youthful appearance. At the age of twenty-six, Harry Guest has already served for several years on active service with his infantry regiment overseas.

First memories are now growing rapidly. At last it dawns on Harry that the year is 1946, not 1942, and that the Second World War has been over for more than a year.

With an effort he tries to stand, but at once feeling queasy, he puts out a hand to steady himself. When he straightens up, he notices for the first time a curious green glow, which constantly varies in intensity; its trembling light is bright enough, and sufficiently constant, for him to make out the massive shape of black rock which inclines, as though designed as a ramp, at an angle of forty-five degrees to the back of the cave, forming a well defined platform which is as smooth and reflective as if polished. He gazes at the oscillating light and listens to the alternate boom and splash of water which is drumming about him. Then, surprised, he recognizes the sound of the sea. Even as he realizes this, in his waking consciousness, he is overtaken by a moment of panic. The tide. The tide is coming in. But, then he understands. The cave entrance must already be under water: when incoming waves burst over the foot of the Bluff outside, the sea must be pouring into the cave, forcing the churning water upwards through the opening, which of course is now below water level; that is the reason for the gushing water as it seethes beneath him. It also explains the reason for the opaque green light which grows alternately stronger and then paler according to the pressure from the sea outside. Light enters the cave when the surface of the pool is lowered by the action of the tide.

Another heavy wave from beyond lifts the water level inside and fills the cave with a pressurized gurgling, followed by a powerful, repeated boom as the pursuing waves break against the headland. This louder noise brings with it a flash of perception; he sees precisely the hopelessness of his situation. As a result of his decision to enter the cave earlier that day, he knows that he is trapped. The water continues to rise, and there is no way of escape.

Part 2:

Cornwall: first visit,

September 1938

"...the place where treasure hath been hid..."

- *The Jew of Malta* - Christopher Marlowe

I

The night was dark. Harry Guest braked his sea-green Hillman Minx at the start of the hair-pin bend leading into the valley and, as he turned, the headlights picked up the first thin wraiths of mist; the moor lay in front of him. At the foot of the hill and following a sharp turn, the road lifted steeply up the valley and the mist thickened. The Hillman was one of the first popular models to introduce synchromesh gears, yet, as he had been taught, Harry double-declutched, and then drove smartly into the mist without slowing down, in spite of the glare of the car's lights as they flattened the mist before his eyes.

At the top of the pass the mist cleared for a quarter of a mile as the road entered the moor, but it returned thicker than ever; suddenly the mist became dense fog and frantically he dimmed the headlights, then turned them off, using sidelights only and braking all the while. But he was driving too fast to control the car as the nearside wheels skidded on the curved edge of the roadside and he felt a jolt. Despite his urgent turn of the wheel and hard acceleration, the car ended up at an acute angle, just short of rolling over, with the offside wheels spinning free and the nearside wheels churning the bog earth and emitting a high-pitched whine like a motorised wood-saw. He tried to reverse but was appalled by the sudden tilt of the car which he thought was about to turn over. And that was it - he was stuck miles from habitation, and yet, as he asked himself, surely not more than ten miles from his destination on the coast. Damn, he said as he switched off the engine and pocketed the keys. Picking up a small satchel containing over-night things, in case he should find somewhere to stay, he climbed out of the car, as the door slammed shut behind him on its own volition, as a result of the steep angle of the vehicle. He could now see that the car was firmly wedged in the ditch. Ten miles was his estimate. Resignedly he started walking across the moor.

Ten minutes later the mist cleared sufficiently for his eye to catch sight of a distant, yellow light, blurred but brilliant on a far-off hillside. Moving towards the light, he soon came across a farm lane at the junction with the tarmacked road. He followed the lane which brought him, after several more minutes, onto a higher plane, where he entered a flood-lit patch of ground bathed in the light which was shed from the downstairs windows of a farmhouse. Looking at the white painted perimeter wall, he saw a gate and the name Moorland Farm. He pushed open the gate and knocked at the front door.

Almost at once the door opened to reveal the slight figure of a dark-haired girl, lit from behind by the yellow light, which shone in his eyes so that he raised his hand to shade them.

"Hello," he said. "I'm awfully sorry to bother you at this time of night, but I've had an accident in my car on the moor. It's wedged in a ditch. Would it be possible for me to use your 'phone for help, please?"

He could not see the girl's face, but he heard the amusement in her voice as she replied, "Going too fast in the mist? You're the same as my brother. But anyway, you can't 'phone. We haven't got one, so you'd better come in and have a word with Mum."

Part 2: Cornwall: first visit, September 1938

Harry stepped inside the lighted hall, brushing against a row of heavy farm coats and capes, hung beneath a variety of caps and hats from a wooden strip with brass hooks fixed to the wall. Stairs mounted to the first floor ahead and to his right an open door revealed the inviting glow of the living room. Before Harry could express his relief and appreciation, the girl said, "My name's Manon. What's yours?"

"I'm Harry Guest, and I'm…"

"Come on then, Mum's in here," she interrupted.

Casting his satchel on a sturdy Victorian table-cum-walking stick stand, he followed her into the bright room, where he at once saw the origin of the vivid light, a paraffin pressure lamp on a round, central table. He also felt the hospitable warmth of a glowing fire after the damp night air. No nonsense about it being a summer evening; the night was cold and so the fire was lit.

Seated by the fire was a thin, white-haired woman with a worried expression on her gentle face. She nodded to Harry to sit in the chair on the far side.

"Good evening, Mr. Guest. I heard what you told Manon. But are you alright? You're not hurt?"

"Thank you. No, just a shake-up. You see. I've only just passed my driving test – and now my Dad's not going to be too pleased. He lent me his car because he thought I was O.K. driving. But the car's not badly damaged. At least I don't think so. It only needs hauling on to the road."

"Nothing to worry about then. Maurice, my son, will get your car clear with the tractor in the morning. He's asleep now. We farmers go to bed early. And I'll be off soon."

Harry had eased himself into the upright wing-backed chair, when she added, "You will have to stay the night. We've got a spare room we keep ready for guests. So you are welcome to have it."

"You are very kind."

Manon called to him from the door. "Would you like a night-cap, Harry? Ovaltine?"

"Yes, please, Manon."

He watched as she turned, saw two dark eyes holding his for a moment, and then the shake of shoulder length hair, the hint of a smile and she was gone.

"Manon didn't tell me your name."

"The family name is Lescaut."

"Is that French?"

"Yes, originally. And we've been farming, mainly cattle, all our lives. As for Manon – she's sixteen – and she has what I call a whimsical name."

"Why do you say whimsical?"

"Well, it was my husband, Jim's idea. But he's away staying the night with his brother in Plymouth."

"And you're not bothered on your own out here?"

"No, no, no. Of course not. I told you Maurice is upstairs and there's Manon, of course. But, about our girl's name. Jim always wanted her to be called Manon. To go with the family name. Do you see? Manon Lescaut. You know, the heroine of the French book by the Abbé Prévost – and of the opera too. He liked the sound of the name and I went along with it. So, that's how it came about. But she's a knowing card."

Harry smiled, "She's very pretty."

Ignoring his remark, she continued, "Oh, I do go on so. Tell me about yourself. Where are you heading?"

"I'm on holiday. I was supposed to get to the Red House above Red Bluff to-night. But that's off now."

Mrs. Lescaut waited as Manon returned with a hot drink for Harry. Then the girl sat on a third, lower chair with knees together, legs splayed awkwardly, her arms crossed on her knees. She was looking into the fire, and Harry for the first time saw the pale, clear skin, the large lips and wide-set eyes – Romney's Emma Hamilton, he thought. She was a beauty.

20

Mrs. Lescaut then asked, "Are you really going to Red Bluff? You'll be seeing our old friends, the Penhalions. Our families have lived in our separate homes for many centuries in this part of the West Country. Their home goes back – what? Four hundred years? Five? It's lovely – and they're great folk."

"I've not met them yet."

"You'll like them. Dan and Jean are the owners of the Red House. And they have a family. Vivian is the eldest and there's Leander, a rather moody lad. But Manon here gets on well with him."

"Mum!" Manon exclaimed. "I don't. I only know him because of the family."

"Oh well, be that as it may. Mr. Guest will be pleased to find their daughter. Alex is a sweet girl with a fine head of auburn-red hair."

"It all sounds super, but what is the Red House like? I heard it was on the coast, but is it actually beside the sea?"

"Oh yes, it's in a spectacular position overlooking Western Cove – and there's a path leading down onto their private beach under Red Bluff itself: that's the headland below the house."

"It'll be a perfect spot. And the weather looks good too."

"So does the coastline. Rugged on both sides of the Bluff and particularly so to the East. There's also a coastal path taking you along the cliff top side. In fact it's always been said there's a lost cave, owned by the Penhalions, although, for my part, I don't believe it ever existed."

"How can a cave be lost?" he asked, smiling.

Mrs. Lescaut laughed. "I mean just that. Nobody in living memory hereabouts has ever found it. It's a manner of speech when I call it a lost cave. The old sayings are hard to die out in Cornwall – and it's still spoken of as if it was there."

She glanced up at the clock on the mantelpiece and cried, "Just look at the time. It's nearly midnight."

To Manon she said, "When Mr. Guest's ready, take him up to the back room. I'll be along in a minute. Well, Mr. Guest, goodnight."

When Harry finished his drink, Manon led the way upstairs, carrying an oil lamp to guide them.

Harry picked up his satchel. He watched the girl, ahead of him in the dancing light. She wore a dark red dress with tightly fitting bodice, a row of six, small, gilt buttons down the front and a high, white, lace collar. Her tiny waist was accentuated by a brown leather belt with a pretty, gilt buckle. For a sixteen year old her hips were surprisingly broad and she moved up the stairs with the agile spring of slim, athletic legs. Her child-like, black shoes were embossed with gilt buckles matching the buttons of her dress. He wondered at the way she was dressed for an evening with her mother at the lonely farmhouse.

At the top of the stairs the landing was lit by another oil lamp which rested on a side table.

"This way," she called, going down a long corridor until she stopped at the far end beside a door which she flung open. She went into the room, placing the lamp on the top of a chest of drawers.

"We keep the bed ready for guests," she explained, "And I slipped up and put a hot bottle, to air the bed for you, while I was getting your drink."

"Thank you very much. You have been kind and I did like talking with your mother."

Harry dropped his satchel on the bed and Manon moved towards the open door.

Suddenly, she swung round so that they faced each other. And then with a swift movement, she stepped forwards, throwing her arms about his neck and holding him to her in a wild embrace. Harry grasped her eagerly, feeling her body pressed against him. She was breathing hard; and momentarily they were still, clinging to each other.

Then Manon turned, and without a backwards glance she left him. He saw the swing of her hair, the straight back, the moving swell of round, young hips as she walked away.

"Manon!" he cried out. But she disappeared round the corner at the end of the passage without saying another word.

II

Harry woke up next day with warm sunshine streaming directly on his face through the open window. As he looked out at the moor, over the farm buildings, he saw the mist had gone. When his eyes returned to the room, he at once recalled the events of the previous night and immediately felt a rising excitement at the memory of Manon. Hastily shaving, washing, dressing, he hurried downstairs, where he found Mrs. Lescaut standing at the open, front door. On hearing his footsteps she turned round.

"Good morning, Mr. Guest," she said. "I hope you slept well. It's a beautiful day. Maurice has been up some time and he's ready to get you on the road again, when you've had your breakfast."

Harry enjoyed his large plateful of sausages, eggs and bacon accompanied by plenty of toast and scalding, black coffee. He looked about him as he ate, into the next room and through the window at the farm, but there was no sign of Manon. Eventually as Mrs. Lescaut cleared the table, he realized that he could no longer put off his departure, and with profuse thanks, he picked up his satchel to go.

"We were lucky to be able to help you. We liked having you, especially as my Jim was away. But now I'll

24

call Maurice and he'll get you on the road in no time with his tractor."

No mention of Manon. She did not appear and Harry now felt certain that she was not going to come.

Within a quarter of an hour he had started the Hillman, thanked Maurice for the tow and was off. Soon after he caught the first smell of brine as he changed gear to drive up to the brow of the ridge on the skyline. The fields were strewn in a haphazard pattern on either side of the road, and now and then he saw wild red fuchsias growing from the base of the grey walls separating the fields. When he steered the car over the ridge, he was unready for the sight which lay before him as far as he could see: rolling, green country, sloping steeply into a fold of land which hid the cliff edge from view, and above the green, the deep, blue sea, glittering with silver flecks under the wide, blue sky where small, white clouds were blown by a brisk, sea breeze.

The Red House Guest House was a long, low building whose first floor windows peeped directly out from under black guttering. A hump-back, grey slate roof, which dipped in the middle, covered the whole building while two tall chimneys balanced each end of the structure. As Harry drove up the track leading to the house, he could see the long shape of what he guessed was Red Bluff, projecting into the bay with the sweep of the two, adjacent coves on either side, framing a ragged, black border of rock. As yet the pale, buff colour of the sand between the sea and the cliff top was still hidden by the ground in between.

Parking the car against a low, greystone wall, he jumped out. The blue front door of the house was open, and the proprietor emerged in response to the sound of car wheels. Dan Penhalion was like a portly farmer wearing a red shirt and thick corduroy trousers, held tightly in place by a leather belt. White hair above red cheeks completed the affable character.

He said, "I'm Dan. We've been worried about you – expecting you last night," but his voice was more anxious than critical.

Harry called out, "I'm very sorry to be late. I had a minor accident on the moor last night."

Dan walked over the gravel and the two shook hands. "You're alright?" he asked.

"Yes, just stuck in a ditch. I stayed the night at Moorland Farm which I found close by, but there was no 'phone. And Mrs. Lescaut put me up. Incidentally she sent you and your family her best wishes."

Dan smiled broadly as he asked, "Ah, yes, they're friends of ours, the Lescauts. But did you meet Manon?"

"Only briefly."

"I bet Mrs. Lescaut told you of her daughter's namesake?"

Harry nodded.

"But what she won't have told you, I'm sure, is that Manon's exactly like her fictitious counterpart – after all the men! Femme fatale, don't you call her, Manon Lescaut?"

Harry felt his cheeks reddening so he quickly turned away, saying, "Yes, you're right", but went on hastily, "Look, come and see the bent mudguard and grazing."

Dan peered over his shoulder.

"That'll soon be put right. Now, let's get you settled in. My wife, Jean, is out with our young daughter, Alex, who's sixteen. And they're visiting a sick friend of ours, but you'll see them when they come back."

"Good. And your sons? I heard there were two".

"Yes. Our Vivian's the eldest, a bit older than you. He'll be in later. But Leander - who was born between the others – he's away. So I'm afraid you'll not be seeing him. He's with a friend."

"Leander. What an interesting name! Was there a reason for choosing it?"

Part 2: Cornwall: first visit, September 1938

"There was. You'll think the Cornish are daft about Christian names – like the Lescaut's daughter. But in our case it wasn't just a whim. He was called after an ancestor living here many years ago."

As he spoke Harry removed his bag and satchel from the car boot and followed Dan into the house and up the staircase to the landing above. Dan opened a bedroom door half-way along as he continued, "The family has lived in this house for centuries, certainly in Elizabethan times. Actually we have an oil painting of the first Leander, a good looking lad. It hangs in the room behind the dining room – nowhere else for it, it's too big. Anyway, have a look at it some time."

Harry was breathing in the sea air at the open window.

Dan said, "You'll be comfy here. Nice sea view. But, I have to give you a warning, which we give all our guests. There are strong currents off the beach on Western Cove which is below Red Bluff. So, it's best to keep well in by the shore if you're swimming. You'll see notices about "NO SWIMMING". But, it's alright if you're careful and don't go out too far. Are you a good swimmer?"

"I think so. I love it. But, I'll be careful."

"Well anyhow, there's safe bathing nearby. You'll find a small, natural pool in the rocks which is excellent for a swim in the heat of the day. And, if you want a drink outside, there's a nice little pub at the local town. Lavington. Called "The Ship"."

Left to himself, Harry unpacked and put away his clothes. He was brushing his hair when he heard the sound of approaching footsteps on the drive. Feminine voices suggested to him that Jean Penhalion and Alex had returned. Curious to see Alex, after Mrs. Lescaut's description of her last night, he hurried on to the landing and down the stairs. As he reached the hall, he met a smiling, sun-tanned woman, plump and good looking, dressed simply in a blue skirt and white blouse. He noticed that there was no trace of grey in her fair hair.

"Hello," she called as she came in through the open door. "You must be Harry Guest. I'm Jean Penhalion. Welcome to our home – and you must call me Jean."

Harry began to explain why he was late arriving, but Jean interrupted him, "No worry. But, I expect you'd like to get out and find your way about Red Bluff and down the beach. I left Alex, who's just gone round to have another go at beating the wall-tennis record. You'll hear her batting against our tennis wall at the back of the house."

"Thanks. I'll see you later."

He went briskly outside and followed a garden path which led towards the sound of racket and ball. When he turned the corner, there was Alex. She was a very pretty girl with shining auburn hair dancing about her shoulders as she played the tennis ball against the wall using firm strokes of her racket. Dressed all in white, shirt and shorts, socks and plimsolls, she was an attractive sight as she moved easily after the bouncing ball, looking young and fresh. For a minute or so he stood watching as she kept the ball going without interruption. But when the ball struck a pebble on the concrete apron in front of the wall, it leapt sideways and she missed it, breaking the spell.

"Bad luck!" called Harry. "That was good."

Alex picked up the ball from the flower bed and hurried over to greet him.

"Hello there. Are you Harry Guest? I'm Alex."

They shook hands, both smiling.

"Sorry to interrupt," said Harry, "but Jean thought you would be free to show me the way to Red Bluff and the surroundings."

"Yes, of course. I've finished here. Just got my best number for uninterrupted strokes – sixty seven. Not too bad."

"I must have a go later, but if you could point me in the right direction, I won't hold you up."

"Come on with me." Alex led him through the garden and down the steps on the path to the headland.

Straightaway the pair were talking together as if they had always been friends.

"What a beautiful place it is!" Harry said, adding, "I'm sorry my parents weren't able to come as they had hoped, but, as Mum explained to Jean on the 'phone, she was called away to take care of her sister, my Auntie Clare. Poor Auntie's recovering from a car accident."

"How is she?"

"Getting on well. But Dad's disappointed. He decided he ought to be with Mum. But he loves Cornwall and will miss it."

As they came to the beginning of the main pathway, they stopped and Alex said, "It's a shame. But, just look at what your Dad loves."

As they descended the hill and started to walk towards the sea, she pointed out the various features she thought he would like to explore: the cliff-edge path to the East; straight ahead up to Red Bluff summit; and Western Cove on the opposite side, leading to a small fishing quay some way along towards St. Minion's point.

"Wonderful!" Harry exclaimed. "And thanks, Alex. I'll have a look round."

"Nothing else?"

"No. It's great to be here."

"Alright. I'll see you later then."

III

N ext day at the Red House Alex was wanted in the kitchen. So Harry decided to go down to the cove. The September sun was hot, cooled by a constant breeze which kept the long grass on the cliff top in perpetual motion. The gulls, cooing mournfully, glided low over the sands and the oystercatchers scuttled across the shore, skilfully avoiding the breaking waves from the incoming tide.

Harry had not forgotten Manon. He realised that she was most likely to be at Moorland Farm, but he hoped to have a chance to see her again on the coast perhaps, or in Lavington which Dan had mentioned. But, as he reached the beach his mind was on the rock pool Dan had also told him about. Running down the shore in search of it, he leaped over the rocks and came out at the top of a rise beside the natural pool itself. When the tide came in, the rocky pool filled with water until it vanished, submerged under the sea. When the tide went out, the sea water spilled in cascades from three sides until the pool was left, brim full and isolated, tempting bathers into its cool basin, scooped smoothly from the jagged rocks. The pool measured some twenty feet across its irregular, oval outline. Although its depth was only about five feet, it made an adequate and secret place for bathing in the sun, always clean, irrigated by the tides. In addition it was secluded, concealed from the beach by a screen of rock and from the Bluff by the overhanging cliff, so that anyone swimming there was only overlooked from the sea.

Casting his eye round, he decided to leave the pool and climb the rocky cliff in search of caves on the near side of the Bluff. As he clambered over the boulders, he reached the smooth sand and skip-jumped to the water's edge, where he sat on a solitary rock. Leaning on his arms and with his bare feet in the foaming sea water, he stared at the incoming sweep of white breakers streaming diagonally towards him.

Then, something caught his attention so that he looked up sharply over his shoulder to his left where the great Bluff stood. On the heights a solitary figure was walking, white skirts flapping about long, brown legs, dark hair flickering in the wind. The lithe, confident walk could only be Manon's. He was immediately on his feet and running up the beach towards the rocks at the far end of the shore, where the sand gave way to the beginning of the headland scrub. Scrambling from rocks to grass, he soon reached the footpath leading to the summit, but when he looked round, Manon was nowhere to be seen. Still, in so short a time she must be up there somewhere. With the certain feeling that she had climbed higher and could not return without his noticing her, he slowed to a steady pace as he strode on. Presently he came to a point where the path split into two ways, one continuing to the side of the bluff, the other rising steeply in the direction of the exposed rim of land, where it ended in a sheer drop to the open sea, beyond the coves on either side. He paused for a minute, feeling the sun burn his face, as he considered which path to take. He calculated that if he went by the top path, he would command the lower ground and therefore he would be able to see Manon if she was below, and if she was above, he would meet her in any case. Accordingly he set off on the higher pathway.

He was halfway to the top, when the path began to turn a corner by a rocky outcrop, where he stopped to glance round at the green finger of land jutting into the swell of the restless sea over to his right. As he stood there a faint sound came to his ears, which caused him to hurry round the bend in the path. There it was again, a girl's laugh. He was sure that it was Manon. Stepping forward he peered down at the lower path. It was a shock to see Manon there with a youth of about his own age. They must have arranged to meet at the spot because they were now lying in each other's arms and rolling on the turf in blissful play. As he watched, the pair tumbled ecstatically and Manon was laughing. Harry felt a disquieting sense of anger mixed with jealousy. He was about to move off, when he stopped on hearing a sharp cry of irritation. As he watched, he saw Manon half rising from the ground. At the same time she pushed the youth, catching him off balance and causing him to fall heavily to one side. In an instant he was grabbing at the long grass in a desperate effort to gain a hold. But he failed, and Harry was horrified to see him slip toward the cliff edge. With a loud shout the youth hung by both hands, clinging to strong tufts of grass. Yet, to Harry's astonishment Manon, still laughing, ran off down the path without looking back.

Harry gauged that the slope, separating the higher from the lower paths at this point was about fifty feet before it fell away sharply. He had no time to use the safer route via the two paths, and so he flung himself across the gap, breaking his sliding fall by gripping wedges of grass as he went. Crossing the lower path he managed to grab one of several, stunted bushes while guiding his body to the point where the frantic stranger hung. He called out, "Hold on."

When he felt the bush which he had grasped would take his weight, he thrust out his free hand.

"Take my hand," he said quietly.

The youth keyed himself to release one hold and seize Harry's extended hand. Then they both clasped hands.

"Well done," he said, looking into the other's eyes. "Now try to bring your foot alongside your arm. Good. That's it."

As the young man lifted one leg and manoeuvred himself, Harry heaved and together they pulled him to safety. It was all over in seconds. Cautiously they heaved themselves back to the lower path.

"Well, that was a near miss," said Harry.

The young man was angry. "Thank you," he gasped as he lay panting. "But, what a devil. Did you see what she did?"

"Yes, I did. I've also met Manon."

"Watch your step with her, don't trust her," he said and under his breath he kept repeating, "The devil."

Eventually when both had recovered, they swapped names. The rescued boy was Philip Tregoran and soon he clambered off with Harry back to the junction of the paths, and impelled by morbid curiosity, up to the Bluff height, where they gazed at the waves dashing against the rocks two hundred feet beneath them, thinking of Philip's close escape.

After a while Harry abruptly put his arm round Philip's shoulder. "O.K.? Are you?" he said, adding, "What about a race to the beach? Do you feel up to it?"

"Of course I do. I'll just show you."

They ran downhill, and Philip reached the sand first.

As Harry drew level, panting, Philip gasped, "There you are." And then, "Thanks Harry, for what you did. I won't forget."

They parted and Harry made his way up to the Red House. When he mounted the last slope, he was pleased to meet Alex. On impulse he said to her, "Can you spare me a minute, Alex?"

Seeing his serious expression, she replied, "Yes, of course. What is it?"

"Nothing, really. But I would like to have a word."

"What? Here?"

"No. In the garden would be better."

Looking puzzled Alex led the way out through the empty living room and the open French windows into the small garden overlooking the sea.

Harry said, "Come and sit for a moment."

There were a number of deck chairs about a teak garden table and they sat together,

"Do you know a local boy called Philip Tregoran?"

"Yes, I do. He's a nice lad. Lives in the next bay and works with his father, Bill Tregoran, at the little fishing quay on the front."

She pointed to indicate its whereabouts further down the coast to the West. "Why do you ask?"

Then Harry told her what had just taken place on Red· Bluff. When he finished, she was quiet for an instant and then she said, "Oh Harry, you could have slipped over the cliff. I know where you were. And poor Philip – how is he?"

"Alright. We had a race down to the beach afterwards."

Alex said, "Oh, you boys! But that girl! I'm not surprised. What a terrible thing to do – to run off like that, when she could see that Philip was in danger of falling off the cliff. She's a bad girl. She has a reputation for leading men on and for blowing hot and cold."

Harry laughed.

"Why are you laughing?"

"I'm sorry. What you said sounded funny coming from you."

Alex blushed and then said, "And now can I ask you something?"

Harry replied, "Yes, of course."

She said, "Please don't tell anybody else about this episode. You see it would upset my parents who are fond of Philip. And it wouldn't help anyway."

Harry answered, "No, of course I won't say anything."

As he finished speaking, Jean's voice could be heard calling her daughter, and so Alex left, saying, "See you later, Harry."

IV

It was not long after Harry's arrival that he spent part of one afternoon with Vivian, tall and slim with curly blonde hair and a bubbly sense of fun. Sun-tanned from spending days on the shore, Harry had climbed from the beach, leaving behind him the Mediterranean-like colours of the sea in the cove, and scrambled up to the Red House.

Pushing open the heavy, back door, he was at first blinded as he came from bright sunlight into the cool atmosphere of the dark corridor. Because of the sudden contrast, he failed to see Vivian approaching and was startled when they collided.

"Sorry!" they said together.

"No bother," Vivian replied. "I'm just going upstairs. Dad wants me to find some old papers he's been binding about for a while now. Told him I'd take a look in the attic. Would you like to join me?"

"Yes, please. Does the attic run the full length of the building?"

"All the way. It's quite a sight, really – and full to the brim with all kinds of junk from donkeys' years past. Come and see."

Vivian started up the stairs and Harry clattered after him to the landing, where Vivian was already opening the ceiling-trap, using a long hooked pole to bring down the folding metal ladder from above. As he disappeared into the attic, Harry followed, clambering from the top step on to a solid floor, constructed from oak planks. Two low-wattage, electric bulbs, one at each end of the long room, cast a pale light into the shadows of the store. As far as he could see in either direction stood furniture of all sizes haphazardly crammed side by side in a vague appearance of order. There were cupboards, shelving, chest of drawers, desks, tables, tallboys, all filling the cavernous space stretching under the length of the old roof. It was hardly a scene of encouragement for the searchers.

"What are we trying to find?" Harry asked. "I mean what's it expected to look like?"

Vivian rubbed his arms and stared round.

"Papers! Could be a file tied with string. Could be stuffed into a cardboard box. Could be anywhere. We'll just have to search. I'll have a go up here – and would you mind looking down the other end?"

"Right, Viv," he answered, turning and walking towards the point indicated. He busied himself opening and closing cupboard doors and drawers, but nothing even promising came to hand. After a while, growing restless in the stuffy air, he picked up a tidy packet, carefully held together with a ragged pink tape. The parcel was wrapped in an old newspaper which had faded into a pale yellow colour and was filthy from years of accumulated dust. Flicking the parcel to clear off some of the dirt, he untied the tape and cautiously opened out the paper. Inside was a set of beautifully designed Georgian fish knives in mint condition. He placed them on a trunk and squatted on a small stool next to it, as he smoothed out the newspaper – and then tried to read the print beneath the grimy surface. Persisting, he was intrigued to see that he was holding a copy of *The Times* newspaper dated 1812. Disappointingly there was nothing of note on the continental war of the period.

Only paragraphs devoted to regional news low down on the page. One of these took his attention with its headline "CORNISH TRAGEDY IN DANGEROUS COVE".

Brushing the paper briskly, he damaged the page which had become soft with age. Exasperated, he propped the surviving pieces against a nearby desk. The press story was brief and appeared under a subheading "From our West Country Correspondent". The reporter wrote of "yet another drowning in the powerful currents which sweep along the local coastline at the point where Red Bluff pushes into the bay. The deceased is the Honourable Sydney Settiscombe, a young man, who it is rumoured, had at the time been seeking to trace a reputed golden treasure among the rocks off Red Bluff". The notice closed with a historical statement recalling the long-held belief in the district that a son of the Penhalion family, who owned a way-side tavern, still in existence, the Red House Inn, was drowned in the same waters in the sixteenth century."

Harry folded the fish knives away in the torn paper and slipped the parcel back where he had found it.

As he peered along the attic, he heard movement from the far end, and called out, "Any luck yet?"

"Yes – at least I think I've got something – in an old biscuit box. Dad'll soon tell me if it's what he wants."

"I found something too." But when Harry described the ancient newspaper story, Vivian's comment was lack lustre.

"Oh, there's always something coming up about hidden gold in the bay. In fact there's something in the Penhalion history, somewhere, I can't remember exactly. It's in a booklet and it's all mixed up with the family's Elizabethan ancestor called Leander – the first Leander, of course – and his connection with the London stage. And, in particular, with the poet-playwright, Christopher Marlowe. He's supposed to have hidden some object along the coast.

But the stories go back across the years and nobody has ever come up with anything."

"What about the Honourable Sydney? Does he mean anything to you? Or the age of the paper – 1812?"

"What about it?" was Vivian's tired reply, but he added quickly, "Honestly, it's just the same old thing we keep getting – details of some poor fellow who drowned in the bay – whatever the year was."

As they prepared to leave the attic, Harry was thinking about the stories. Old Mrs. Lescaut had first spoken of what she called a "lost cave", and she must have been repeating what others had believed down the years.

In The Times' account the words "gold treasure" had been used, but only referred to this gold being "amongst the rocks off Red Bluff", nothing more specific. What about "lost cave"? A cave seemed a much more likely place to hide treasure, in all sorts of fissures and gaps in the rocks. More secret too. Anything left amongst rocks sounded all too easy to find – and much less likely to be in place still. And why risk your life at the well-known danger spot in the bay, unless you truly believed that something valuable lay there to be discovered – the lure of gold? In the case of the Honourable Sydney, he may well have had more reason than was known to suspect the presence of gold.

Vivian was descending the steps noisily, so Harry went after him, turning off the attic lights as he joined him below.

V

Harry was oblivious to time passing in the hot summer days. One afternoon after changing, he left his bedroom and at the same time glimpsed the half-open door at the end of the landing. He had often noticed it and wondered why it was never closed. What lay beyond the door? On impulse he went over and peered into the room. Facing him was a closed window which shed light enough to see round. It was obviously a dumping place for anything not wanted by the family for the time being – and perhaps not ready yet for promotion to semi-permanent residence in the attic.

Really, he could see that the room was not unlike a run-down junk shop. A large kitchen table in the centre was covered with a litter of extraordinary and differing objects: coloured vases, a dim-surfaced copper kettle, ten or more leather-bound books in a careless pile, a tall china candle stick which had been converted into a table lamp with a wide orange shade, the latter filthy with dust, and several boxes mixed up with discarded cooking utensils. It was a complete muddle. In contrast a bookcase stretched across the opposite side of the room, covering the wall from floor to ceiling; the shelves were filled with books, apparently in apple-pie order. Fortunately a broad passage separated the packed bookcase from the table, so that he could get comfortably between them as he carefully examined the books. A thoughtful hand at sometime had arranged them by subjects under authors' names in alphabetical order. Casually he picked out several books one after another, glancing through the pages before returning each one to its original space. There were volumes of classical fiction, poetry, history, mainly of Great Britain and North Ireland, biography and all kinds of miscellaneous items and curiosa. Suddenly a title caught his eye amongst the cloth covers, perhaps partly because the book was bound with a plain, buff-coloured covering, which stood out amongst the other colours. Harry pulled it from the shelf.

Inside the book he saw that it had been printed privately for the Penhalion family by Maxwells of Plymouth in 1850. It was a fussy, rather conceited publication filled with minute and fascinating historical observations concerning the fashionable dress, behaviour, seasonal activities and events running down the years and set out with innumerable stories and anecdotes dating back to Tudor days and forward to Victorian times. In fact it was a miniature family history. Flicking through the pages, he stopped occasionally to read passages and then turn on to find more. In this way he came across a piece describing the early years of the Red House, when it had first been established as a tavern called The Red House Inn. Were there any other volumes? There was no indication to confirm this possibility. The literary "etchings" had the appearance of being assembled from past memoirs and diary descriptions and letters, all handed down from generation to generation over the years – and now brought together in historical order at the date of printing.

Among the stories Harry read of the Penhalion family's eldest son, in the reign of Queen Elizabeth I, who was called Leander.

This is more like it. It should be really interesting, he thought, to know what was recorded about the first Leander. He was said to be an exceptionally handsome young man, but he was considered too effeminate to knuckle down to the fishing trawls of the other men from local shore-line families. In any case the report stated he always wanted to become an actor, having heard first-hand tales from sailors, who had served in vessels calling at the Port of London, about the many theatres by the River Thames. And so, nobody was surprised when Leander left home to make his way to London, where he cleverly managed to join the famous company of players called "The Admiral's Men", the distinguished troupe of Lord Howard, the Lord Admiral, who was Lord Howard of Effingham and the Queen's cousin. The troupe was furthermore privileged to perform many of the plays written by the phenomenal young playwright and poet, Christopher Marlowe. In due course, Marlowe and Leander met and shortly the two became inseparable friends. Indeed it was always supposed that Marlowe changed the Penhalion boy's name to Leander, because, at their first meeting the poet was in the process of writing his poem – which was never completed – and which was called "Hero and Leander". Marlowe liked the name Leander so much, and as he became so fond of the boy, he always used the name Leander for him. And the name had stuck.

Harry paused to slap the pages of the book against his hand to disperse some of the accumulated dust. When he looked at the book, he tried to find other details of Marlowe, amazed by what he had read. Marlowe, the report went on, was always in trouble. The worst, in these troubled times, was his alleged atheism, but it was also rumoured that he had stolen a masterpiece of Italian art. The latter most beautiful object had somehow come into Marlowe's hands, complete with a special casket, designed for its protection.

This was all supposed to have happened during a visit Marlowe made to Holland.

However, later on when intense rumours were going round concerning Marlowe's alleged blasphemy, the poet became afraid that his lodgings in London could be searched by the authorities, seeking evidence, and the masterpiece could be discovered.

Leander and Marlowe were closely bonded friends by now; and so without a second thought Leander at once volunteered to hide the precious object in the place which he believed to be the safest on earth, situated within sheltered rocks, in a secret part of the shore near to his old home above high cliffs in Cornwall. But, the beckoning story came to a tantalising close. It simply stopped after reporting that Leander Penhalion was thought to have drowned in dangerous Cornish waters in 1594.

Very, very interesting. Harry returned the old book to its place on the shelf, and as he did so, a memory returned to him of the day recently when Vivian – while they were together in the attic – had said something about a family history. At any rate the details added rich colour to the other strands of local history which he had collected. And yet, there was never anything firm, nothing absolute – "sheltered rocks" for example was a pretty vague clue to go on, and that was the very last phrase to appear.

VI

It was the end of the holiday. Tomorrow Harry would return home. Meanwhile the 23rd September brought with it gales. Harry had been wakened in the night by the bang of a swinging window, but he did not get up to shut it and stayed in bed listening to the wind screeching through the driven trees about the drive. In the morning the wind had dropped slightly, but, as he peered out of the open, bedroom window, he could see clouds streaming past, dull grey, tinged with a purple streak. Even the sea had lost its blue, changed now to green and bearing slow, majestic lines of breakers steadily over the water from far out.

After breakfast Harry pulled on an old shiny black mac, which he borrowed from the garments hanging by the hall door. As he stepped outside he leaned into the gusty wind, intent on exploring the two coves on either side of the Bluff more thoroughly than he had done to date.

Vivian, at the beginning, had told him about the dinghies, owned by the family, urging him to make use of them. As he had said they were always berthed on a rise above Western Cove beach, where there was a flat rock surface, surrounded by boulders so that the boats were well sheltered from winter storms. In Edwardian times the Penhalion family had enjoyed boating for pleasure from this point where they had blasted grooves to take the sturdy timbers, which they had sunk in place to support a substantial, hand-operated winch. By means of a cable, which had to be attached to the stern of a boat, the winch was used alternately for lowering boats along the gradual, rock slope and later for drawing them up again to the berths above. The family kept the winder and the beams in good repair, just as their predecessors had done before them. Subject to the state of the tide and the condition of the sea, dinghies could either be launched into the sea or dragged a few yards along the sand to the water's edge.

Harry planned to take out one of the dinghies in the afternoon, hoping that the wind would subside sufficiently for him to do this when the time came. He wanted to try to row round into the neighbouring cove. By taking a look at the rocky Bluff from the sea, he believed that he might observe something – he did not know what – perhaps the shape of rock strata which could indicate the possibility of the opening of a cave. Unfortunately as it was the last day of the holiday, this was his last chance too, at least until next year.

Within an hour the sun shone through the melting clouds and the wind dropped further to a milder but steady breeze as Harry had wished; with this change the rich, blue colour returned to the sea. Dressed in white shorts and red shirt under his black mac, he slung his satchel across his shoulders. It contained his lunch, coffee and a powerful torch. He sat now beside the dinghies. One was painted red and white and on its side was the name Jack in black letters, and the other was painted blue and white with Jill, also in black letters, along the side of the bow. They were small and light, each made for two people. Harry ate his sandwiches and drank the hot, sweet coffee. As he watched the waves breaking on the sand, he realised that it was low tide and as far as he could judge, it was much lower than usual.

It was at this fortuitous moment that a fisherman came into view, climbing in a leisurely fashion over the nearby rocks and making his purposeful way towards Harry. When he got within hailing distance, Harry called, "Hello there! May I ask you to give me a hand, please?"

The sailor, who wore thick, black serge trousers and a navy blue sweater with 'Sea Queen' sewn in white letters in a curve across his chest, lumbered up with his plodding walk. On his head was an aged, sailor's cap, badge in front and white canvas on top. Under the cap his face was dark brown and lined.

In his soft Cornish accent he said, "I want to see you. My name is Bill Tregoran."

"Oh, good afternoon, Mr. Tregoran. I met your son on Red Bluff the other day."

"No, you call me Bill like everyone else. And I take it you're Harry Guest."

"That's me."

"And I wanted to say something to you." He eased himself up against the side of Jill and took a puff at his pipe. "I'm not going to say much. But I lost my old Nell, Phil's mother, a year ago and so you see Phil is all I have in the world. And I want to thank you for saving his life, as you did, up there." He pointed to the Bluff.

Harry said, "We were both lucky. It was lucky I was there, and anybody would have jumped to it."

Bill brushed his remarks aside, "Not anybody. And you could have slipped over too. No, I know what was done. But there's another thing I want to ask: you haven't told anybody about it, have you?"

"Only my friend, Alex Penhalion, at the Red House. And she won't talk about it. She said she wouldn't."

Bill looked at him squarely. "That's good. I tell you why. My Philip wouldn't stand a chance with that young witch."

"Manon?"

"Yes, young Manon, I call her a witch. And if the story got around, you can guess what she would say happened on Red Bluff, can't you?" Bill did not wait for an answer, "She'd say she'd been attacked and was defending herself."

"But I saw..." Harry began.

"Never mind that. It's best that the episode is forgotten. And Phil will learn from it. That's all I wanted to say. Thank you, lad."

"Thank you Bill. Of course I won't say anything. But would you help me launch Jill, please?"

"What do you want to go out in this swell for?"

"It's my last day of holidays and I want to have a look at the Bluff from the sea."

"Well, you mind how you go."

"Can you tell me if the tide's very low – it seems to be?"

"Yes, it is. You know what it is – you know the time of year?"

"No."

"What do they teach you at School? It's the time of the Autumn Equinox – and it's the twenty third of September. You know that?"

"Yes, I do, but I didn't connect the date with today. And, there's a Spring Equinox too, isn't there?"

"You've got it. It's when the sun crosses the equator. And each year on that date the tides – all over the world – are at their lowest. The Spring tide's on March 21st and it's called the Vernal Equinox."

"Are the tides at their lowest beyond those two precise dates every year?"

"Yes, but only for a day or so, I believe."

They chatted on and as time passed the wind dropped even more, so that Harry commented on the change.

"That may be," replied Bill. "But she'll be blowing again by nightfall. You see. Well, I've got to get on. Glad to have found you. And now I'll give you a hand before I go."

Together they launched Jill, slipping her down the shore and into the sea. Bill left with a wave of his pipe. Harry meanwhile soon had the dinghy under control, leaning strongly on the oars until he was well clear of the beach. Bill was already far off, on the way back to his quay.

It took Harry some twenty minutes of hard rowing to get the boat out into the bay, adjacent to the Bluff, where he could feel the strong pull of the treacherous, cross currents. He rowed on enjoying the feel of salt water spraying his face and the wind fussing at his hair. As he pulled, he entered a choppier stretch and the dinghy took in water which splashed over the stern. Presently he rested, letting the dinghy toss against the buffeting waves.

Staring upwards, he saw the menacing shape of the giant cliff front. At its head the Bluff formed a pincer, two arms projecting as if to protect the dark cove in between.

Harry was still some way off when he changed course and rowed in a parallel line with the cliff, intending to close in for an inspection, when suddenly his eye caught the outline of a low archway set in the base of the rocks near the centre of the pincer cove. As he stared the arch disappeared in the swell of the sea and then it returned to view. Excited, he pulled strongly on the oars for several minutes but making slower progress, until at last when he turned to look back under the towering cliffs, he saw it distinctly. It was the entrance to the cave, inky black at the core, low and wide, constantly splattered and obliterated by the frothing sea, but visible. He now put his back into a final effort, rowing fiercely. But when he turned again, the cave had vanished as if it had never been there. Sunk in disappointment he rowed back and forth for some while but to no avail. He could find no trace of the cave any more. Manoeuvring the dinghy for the return journey, he discovered how dangerous the sea off Red Bluff could be: with great difficulty he managed to row clear of the rocks and there followed a long, hard pull to the beach, where he could see that the tide had now turned. He hauled the boat off the waves and then went for the cable. Returning, he fixed the cable to the boat and ran back to winch Jill up to the berth beside the other dinghy.

As he was walking up to the Red House, on a whim he crossed the grassy slope away from the path. Sauntering along, he caught sight of a black shape, hidden amongst dense creeper in a hollow in the ground. Curious, because he had not seen it before, he drew nearer and was surprised to find that it was an old, storage shed, made of thick, tarred wood with a cobwebbed window in the side facing the sea. It was camouflaged by nature and it merged with the countryside, as if it was rock showing through undergrowth. There was no visible sign of a path to the shed, which looked as though it was no longer in use. Satisfied, he returned to the path leading up to the house.

As he arrived at the top of the slope he met Alex. The two chatted until presently their talk turned to the subject of Leander. This prompted Harry to tell Alex how he had found the family's records book with its reference to the first Leander. Alex eagerly commented.

"Yes," she said. "It's all been a part of our family story. But I've only glanced through the book – I'm sorry to say – years ago, and I've not seen it lately. Well done you. I must have another look at it."

She smiled and then asked, "By the way, have you seen Leander's portrait yet?"

"No. Your father did mention it when we first met. But, please tell me about it."

"It's a lovely thing and a genuine antique, one of the family's few treasures."

"And you are saying that the picture dates from Elizabethan times. Well over three hundred years – more?"

"True, and it's in pretty good shape. A bit dark of course with dust and grime over the years. But, it's so

Was There Ever Seen Such Villainy?

like my brother. When he looks at the painting, he could be staring into a mirror. That's how much alike they are. Come on. I'll show you."

She hurried ahead of him and opened the door. They entered a room whose sombre ceiling was amber coloured. There was a slightly musty smell inside. In front of them, dominating the whole space, hung a large picture in an aged ebony frame, decorated with intricate gold scrolls superimposed on the woodwork. Standing before it, Harry studied the portrait of a beautiful young man dressed in a golden tunic with white ruffs and cuffs. His long hair gave him an effeminate appearance and his thin mouth and eyes, just too close together, suggested a weak character. Harry was intrigued by the thought that he was looking back in time over the centuries into the vivid eyes of the first Leander Penhalion. "What do you think?" Alex asked.

"It's really splendid. The ruff and the tunic make him seem stronger than his expression suggests, not altogether masculine... And the deep reds and golds lighting the tunic..."

"Yes. But, there's something else for you to see. Let's have the picture down."

Together they lifted the heavy frame from the wall and turned it round, propping it up carefully. There was a notice fixed to the reverse side which had been written out in a clear, elegant hand. It read as follows:

"This oil painting, by an anonymous artist, is believed to date from the sixteenth century. Tradition has it that the picture is the portrait of one, Leander Penhalion, of the one-time Red House Inn at Red Bluff in the Duchy of Cornwall, England."

Lower down on the piece of paper the writer had copied out some lines from Christopher Marlowe's unfinished poem *Hero and Leander*:

"Some swore he was a maid in man's attire,

50

For in his looks were all that men desire, -
A pleasant-smiling cheek, a speaking eye,
A brow for love to banquet royally;
And such as knew he was a man, would say,
'Leander, thou art made for amorous play;
Why art thou not in love, and lov'd of all?
Though thou be fair, yet be not thine own thrall."

"It is said to have been painted at the time when Leander Penhalion joined the Lord Admiral's Players in London, where he became the close friend of Christopher Marlowe, poet and playwright."

When Harry had finished reading it, he said, "Whoever wrote that must have seen the family history book. Perhaps it was the same person who wrote the book." He turned the picture round so that they could see it again.

"We don't know who the writer was. But Dad thinks it was probably written by an ancestor, perhaps early in Queen Victoria's reign."

"I agree with your Dad." He read the notice once more and stared at the portrait.

Alex interrupted his thoughts. "I'm sorry, Harry. I must go. Kitchen chores."

Before going up to his bedroom, Harry remained quite still. As he gazed at Leander's handsome face, he felt curiously moved by what he perceived to be an insolent expression showing beneath the look of bright intelligence which the artist had caught dramatically. Alex's young brother was generally thought to be exactly like the portrait, but Harry disliked the character he saw portrayed. While he wondered what the Leander of to-day would be like, he could not suppress an uneasy feeling that trouble lay ahead between the two of them.

Shaking off the thought, he replaced the picture on the wall with difficulty on his own. Then he ran upstairs to get ready to join the family for the farewell dinner.

The Penhalions had placed three bottles of wine in line down the centre of the table on the white linen table cloth.

Dan was speaking. "Mr. Chamberlain's off to meet Adolph Hitler. It's gathering war clouds, I'm afraid – and so soon after the Great War. Let's hope he's successful in bringing peace back with him."

"Oh, don't let's talk about politics!" exclaimed Jean. "Let's enjoy the evening with Harry. It may be sometime before he's back in Cornwall again."

"I hope I can get back next year," Harry said. "It's been such a super holiday."

"What did you do today?" asked Alex.

"I rowed out under Red Bluff."

"In this gale?"

"Oh, it wasn't too bad. But, do you know, I thought I saw the outline of a cave at the foot of the headland."

Vivian was quick to say, "Not possible, old boy. You must have been mistaken. I've grown up here and I've never seen one at that point. Have you, Dad?"

Dan paused from serving the meal to answer. "No. No, I've never seen one, but that's not to say one doesn't exist. But I think you must be mistaken, Harry. What were the conditions like?"

"There was a fair swell on and it was a rough row. Jill took in a lot of water. But I saw the opening several times and once quite clearly. Of course there was a lot of spray, and movement of the dinghy, so I could have been mistaken, but…"

Jean joined in. "As you know, over the years there's been a tragic loss of life in those waters, out there between the two coves, what with the submerged rocks and those devilish currents. Many people have been drowned. Don't go out when it's rough if you return next year, dear."

Harry went on brightly. "There was a lull in the gale at the time and Bill Tregoran warned me that it would get worse in the evening, so I took my last chance. But he was right." His last words referred to the rattling windows and the stirring curtains in the room, as the wind penetrated the woodwork's cracks and rain lashed the glass outside.

To Harry's surprise even Alex was against him. She said, "It's just not likely, Harry, after all these years. Mum and Dad would surely have known – and all the people living locally too. Maybe it was a trick of the light playing on the sea – combined with the movement of the dinghy and the breaking waves on the cliff, all could have created the illusion." She smiled, softening her words.

But Harry dropped the issue without more comment. He was sure that he had seen the mouth of a cave. The strong memory stayed with him until the time when he could return to the Red House.

Part 3:
Return to Cornwall:
September 1946 and to
the end of the year

FERNESE: What wind drives you thus into Malta-road?

BASSO: The wind that bloweth all the world besides,
Desire of gold.

- *The Jew of Malta* - Christopher Marlowe

I

Because of petrol rationing, it had been impossible to run the sea-green coloured Hillman Minx during the war. Consequently the car had rested on wooden blocks for a total of nearly seven years, but it was back on the road as good as new and with only a small mileage on the clock. The car was responding to Harry's ebullient mood as he sped across the English countryside; he had deliberately taken an out-of-the-way route for his journey to Cornwall, driving across the centre of Dartmoor via Dunsford, where he swung along the snaking road which threads up the gorge to Moretonhampstead and finally on to the edge of the moor itself. Passing the old sign beside a small, roadside garage - "Last petrol before the Moor"- he began switch-backing over the fabulous moor, pausing for a delicious pint of beer at the Warren Arms in the centre, and on to the Red House in Cornwall.

As he approached the ridge before the sea, he was surprised by the strong emotions which took hold of him. He suddenly realised that the view, lying on the far side of the hills, somehow symbolised not just his return to Cornwall but more particularly his safe return from the war. Yet, nothing had prepared him for the sensation which he experienced as the car crossed the rim of the hills; and he saw again the breathtaking view of the royal blue sea, the white surf and the silver flashes of sunlight on the surface of the water. At that moment he was struck by the full realisation of how fortunate he was to have survived the war; and he remembered close friends who had not been so lucky. The words of the last verse of an old Eighth Army song came into his head:

"And now, we are way back in England.
The war, it is over and won.
But, remember the pal left behind you,
Who was shot by the old Iti gun."

He pulled up so as to gaze at the scene, car windows wide open and the fresh breeze from the sea blowing in his face. After several minutes he drove down to the Red House.

There was excitement at his arrival in the house, where with cries of welcome the older Penhalions stepped out to meet him, on hearing his car. When the greetings were over, they hurried inside and then out and over to the white painted bench seat in the sun by the dwarf wall. Dan and Jean were both whiter haired now but brimming with good health, Dan's red cheeks and Jean's brown face in sharp contrast, just as Harry remembered them eight years ago.

Jean said, "The others will all be here for dinner, Vivian, Leander and Alex. Viv's on leave. He's a Major with the Buffs and he was awarded the M.C. for action in North Africa. Our Leander stayed with us in his reserved, farming occupation. He was taken on by the Lescauts at Moorland Farm, where you stayed on that first night. Do you remember?"

"Yes, of course I do. And Mrs. Lescaut?"

Dan answered seriously, "It was sad. She was killed in an air raid. You wouldn't think it possible, but she was determined to visit her sister in Plymouth – and that's where it happened."

"Oh, I am sorry. I really liked her."

"And her husband, Jim, was devoted to her. He never got over it and he died quite recently. The son Maurice was reserved on the farm, and he's taken over from his father."

Harry asked, "And Manon?"

Jean replied, "She's alive and kicking. She's home now, I think – in fact you may see her. She was in the WRENS. Alex is up at Moorland Farm with Leander and Maurice. Alex is in the Land Army, and she's working up there, more part-time now. But when we get the Guest House properly on its feet again, she will be in helping us to run it. In fact she'll be with me during your visit." She smiled, "But enough of us, what about you? Here I am talking about us in Cornwall…"

"My army unit became a parachute regiment. At present – since my discharge – I've been assisting in my father's London office. But I've got a place at Cambridge in October, when I'll have to get down to it after all these years."

At this point they heard the engine of what proved to be a bull-nosed Morris. Harry sprang to his feet.

"Go on," urged Jean. "It's the family."

In the drive Harry saw the three occupants of the Morris climbing out. Vivian, smartly clothed in brown tweed sports jacket, shirt and tie with dark grey slacks and polished shoes, was giving a hand to his sister, Alex, in her green sweater of the Land Army and buff coloured breeches, looking stunning in the sunshine. The third figure, bronzed and dressed in old corduroys and woollen shirt, hung back. Harry had not met Leander, but as soon as he saw the young man's feminine, good looks, he recognised him as being identical in appearance to the portrait in the back room which he had seen so long ago.

Vivian and Alex rushed forward and Alex kissed Harry as Vivian slapped him on the shoulder. "Are you coming to The Ship with us tonight?" he asked as one determined to settle first things first.

Harry laughed. "Yes, please."

Before dinner Harry was taken with the three younger Penhalions to The Ship, while Dan and Jean insisted on staying to prepare the welcome-home dinner party. The four wedged themselves into the Morris. Vivian drove swiftly and competently on to the coast road and five miles down to the small town of Lavington, where the ancient inn had been built in the mid-fourteenth century. The pub sign was hard to discern as it badly needed painting, but it was still possible to make out the image of a ship in a heavy sea.

They pushed their way inside noisily. There were two bars contained under a low and yellowed ceiling; it was dark inside and the floor consisted of large flagstones which must have dated back to Chaucer's day. From the neighbouring, saloon bar came a hub-bub of talk, although it was impossible to get a clear view of the drinkers there, because a number of movable, quarter lights were suspended on a wooden frame between the two bars. The public bar, where Harry's party settled, was however empty. Vivian ordered a round of drinks.

As the evening progressed, Leander became more cheerful but never forthcoming, as if he felt shy, or perhaps even resentful of the fact that Harry and Vivian had been in action in the war, while he had been at home on the farm. They were all seated about a long table on one side of which was a high, black painted settle, where Alex and Vivian sat with their backs to the bar. Leander perched on one end of a form, his back also to the bar, while Harry balanced on the other end of it, from where he could see the old barman and sometimes the shapes and faces of the rowdy party.

Vivian had been wounded and then captured before eventually escaping from Germans of the Afrika korps in the desert. He was telling a story about how Rommel, courteous and correct, had visited him with other allied prisoners of war in a German Desert Hospital, thoughtfully enquiring about their conditions and speaking in excellent English. As the tale unfolded, Harry looked up and noticed a dark-haired girl as her head was suddenly framed in two of the quarter lights; the girl tossed her hair back from her face in an action which he recalled from his memory of that single night years ago; it was Manon. She was wearing a simple, white shirt and blue skirt and on each side of her – as he could see by moving his head slightly – were two naval officers. As he stared, she turned, conscious of his intent gaze, an amused smile barely perceptible at the corners of her mouth as she showed that she had recognised him.

Harry bought another round of drinks and somebody else bought another, until Alex insisted that it was time to go home. Singing Eighth Army songs, they were driven safely and cheerfully back to the Red House. As wine was scarce, they had brought back flagons of beer from the pub, and this was poured out repeatedly. The conversation was so lively that even Leander laughed. When it came to retiring to bed, Harry felt benevolent and full of drink.

After happy "goodnights" on the landing, he entered his bedroom, the same one as on his last visit, and closed the door, leaning against it as he recalled the excitement of the reunion. Shortly after, he took a step forward, meaning to cross the room and draw back the curtains to look at the sea under the stars, but as he did so, he tripped and found himself falling heavily across the bed. He managed to twist so as to avoid striking his head, but his right shoulder crashed against the wall with the full thirteen stones of his body's weight. He lay still at first to clear his head and also to see if anybody had heard the fall, but there was silence elsewhere, so he concluded that the thick wall had deadened the bump. However, there had been another sound, when he hit the wall, the noise of falling plaster. He groaned when he thought of the mess to clear up and the damage which he must have caused. As the seconds passed, he gently eased his arm round at the socket, but to his relief the initial pain was already receding, and as he rose gingerly to his feet, stretching his arms, he was satisfied that he had escaped with no more than a shaking. But he must examine the wall. Lowering himself on his hands and knees, he peered under the bed, but there was no sign of any loose plaster. Frowning, as he considered what this meant, he glanced up at the wall. A strange sight it was too. It looked as if part of the wall had come adrift at the centre point, because a whole section appeared to have opened up like a cupboard door, and for a moment he thought that he must have come upon a secret hiding place. On looking more carefully, he saw that the ancient wall had obviously been papered over repeatedly, layer on layer, sheet upon sheet, over the years until its texture had become as strong as papier mache and as thick as cardboard. The thick wallpaper had covered over the lathe-plaster, and the latter had smashed on the impact of his fall. At the same time the broken pieces had plunged into the inside of the wallpaper which was strong enough, lower down, to retain them at the bottom. That was why there was no mess on the floor, and it also explained what had caused the rattling sound which he had heard. He noted that, curiously, there was no dent in the wallpaper, where his shoulder had landed. Presumably the shattered plaster had absorbed the blow.

He quietly eased the bed away from the wall. Next, he cautiously fingered the paper to investigate the extent of the damage, but he gained the impression that the paper could be pressed back without ever showing that there had been a fracture behind. He examined the dark cavity, revealed by the opened, paper strip, and then moved the bedside lamp so that its orange light was cast into the gaping space. It was then that he noticed something like a piece of dirty paper protruding from the shattered plaster. Inserting his thumb and index finger, he pulled, as carefully as possible so as not to tear it, and eventually he removed a folded document, consisting of several sheets of aged paper. Slowly he opened it up.

It was a letter. At the top, on the right hand side of the first sheet, he could see the date: 30th June, 1593.

II

E very sign of the evening's drinking evaporated. Harry's head became clear and alert as he concentrated on the letter, excited at his accidental discovery. First of all, however, he pressed the stiff wallpaper back against the wall, where it fitted as if it had hardly been disturbed. Then he moved the bed into place, propped himself up, using a pillow upright behind his shoulders, and began to read through the yellowed pages. Some words were almost obliterated by time and dust; others were puzzles of handwriting to be deciphered; and over-all there were difficulties of writing usage of the period. He persisted to the end. When he glanced at the clock on the mantelpiece, he was surprised to see that an hour had passed since he started reading. Feeling weary, he flattened his pillow, placed the letter on his bedside table, turned out the light and fell asleep at once.

In the morning he awakened early.

Sunshine poured in between the curtains. After his fall, he had forgotten to open them, so he sprang out of bed and flung them apart. The sun was bright and he stood watching the sea birds drifting across the wide, blue sky as he listened to the cry of the gulls.

Part 3: Return to Cornwall: September 1946

Purposefully he returned to bed bringing with him a pen and a notebook, which he always carried in his jacket pocket. His mind had slipped back to his school days, when he was working for Higher Certificate English History. He remembered vividly that enthralling account of 'The History of the Great Rebellion', written by Edward Hyde, Earl of Clarendon, during the 1640s; and he recalled too that his form's copy of the work used a text with simplified reading for modern students; the punctuation and in particular the spelling and, when necessary the prose, had all been brought up-to-date without altering the sense of the classic history. He decided that it was going to be a lot easier to concentrate on the contents of the letter if he copied it in a similar fashion. So, for the next hour, he worked out in his notebook his own, modernised draft from the original text.

The draft of the letter is as follows:

"To – Sydney Penhalion
The Red House Inn, in the Duchy of Cornwall
30th June 1593
Father,

The matters of which I write are of signal importance to me at a time when my fate is poised between the Scylla of the Privy Council's activities and the Charybdis of the guardian tides in the approaches to Red Bluff point.

But, first and foremost, alas, I bear the most terrible and tragic news of the fate of my Master and dearest friend, Kit Marlowe, who has perished – or more precisely who was foully murdered - in Deptford Strand at Eleanor Bull's tavern on the night of the 30th May. He it was, you will recall, who – arising out of his poem entitled *Hero and Leander* (the one which he never completed) – named me Leander too, believing that I resembled that one, Leander of his poem (leastways in his mind's eye) and thus was I known and called amongst each one of my colleagues of the Lord Admiral's Players.

It is therefore with a heavy heart, and also with greatest fear, for reasons which I shall shortly hope to show, that I write presently and in greatest urgency on two separate counts, as I have indicated above. In the event that I should die, or be done to death by either or any other cause, I hope through you, my Father, and by the instrument of this letter, to provide for the future security of a special treasure, namely one which is a supreme example of the goldsmith's art. I therefore purpose to set out as follows in exact detail the whereabouts of the aforementioned Masterpiece which could otherwise be forever lost from the sight of man."

It is an extraordinary story. And, from the way he writes, the young Penhalion has grown up quickly, sorting himself out and getting to London in spite of the many travelling hazards in those days. How did he get there: via Plymouth and then by working his way on ship-board? Joining the Admiral's Men, the leading Company of Players, was surprising in view of his apparent lack of experience. But the Troupe must have been impressed by his enthusiasm and intelligence – and perhaps by his natural acting ability. Certainly by his staying power. Still – memories of history at school – actors in Elizabethan days faced a daunting routine: each day there would be rehearsals for new plays in addition to rehearsing current productions – together with the perpetual memorising of lines. And an actor could have up to thirty different parts committed to memory! What a determined Elizabethan he was!

"My tale commences in the year 1591, when Kit Marlowe was working closely with a goldsmith, one Poole (whom he had met in Newgate Prison in 1589) with whom he was experimenting in the forging of gold coins – and mighty circumspect were they both in the certain knowledge that the fate of the convicted counterfeiter is immersion in boiling oil. However, together, they endeavoured to pass some such of their forged coins in the country of Holland during the month of January in the following year. Unfortunately they were caught out in their enterprise in January 1592, and yet – by the most amazing good fortune – they escaped condemnation on account of the fact that they could in no way have truly hoped to pass the coins without the coins' true value being immediately recognised. Their excuse – that they were pretending to pass forged coins with humorous intent – was accepted by the authorities, although the event and its outcome were, to my way of thinking, surely a close run thing.

It was later on that Kit Marlowe met another and more accomplished goldsmith, one Thomas Williams, who duly forged a set of most superior coinage, gold Gelders, which were used for the purchase of the said Masterpiece in Holland."

What sort of man could Kit Marlowe have been! What a desperately irresponsible risk to take – even for gold. To think of going into a plot – with eyes wide open to the possibility of meeting the ghastly consequences of the crime, if his attempt to pass more forged coins had been discovered! To modern eyes the very idea was surely too appalling to contemplate: this time the certain punishment must be immersion in boiling oil as the form of execution laid down.

How would anybody feel if faced with being propelled towards the place of execution on the ordained day? Perhaps walking bare footed towards the vast, waiting metal cauldron, glowing at the end of a dark cellar and exuding a powerful glow of heat. And the sound, too, hardly heard at first, of irregular plopping from the bubbling surface of oil. Then, as his footsteps bring him nearer to the source of the sizzling oil, the retching as the stench of the horrendous brew reaches his nostrils. How could the poet have taken such a risk? Another pace and he is beside the great vat, and he notices that the chamber's flagstone floor, which at first felt damp, is now dry and the atmosphere is hot from the metal glowing brightly orange-red at the base of the cauldron. At last the moment arrives; he climbs the strong, wooden steps leading to the brink, to the time of death, when his naked body will slip from the powerful hands of his two massive guardians into the seething oil, his arms already closely secured by tarred rope.

The law is determined to defend society from the cruel crimes committed by the forger – and also by the poisoner – with, in those days, the terrifying threat of the boiling oil execution, on the grounds, I suppose that both crimes are more dangerous than others because they are the hardest to detect. But, how could Kit have escaped execution earlier and seem to go free? Was there some power behind him? How could the mystery of Kit Marlowe otherwise be explained?

"It should at this stage be clarified that Kit Marlowe had for some time worked as a secret agent – as he informed me alone – within the vast spy ring organised by Sir Francis Walsingham, who bears the title of Her Majesty's Secretary of State. Kit Marlowe's secret appointment to Sir Francis Walsingham's service made it possible for him to voyage across the Channel to The Hague from time to time, so that coincidentally he was able to chance upon the demi-world of those engaged in the sale and purchase of artistic treasures through European markets, which are well established there. In due course Kit Marlowe made contact by this means with a Dutchman, one Jan de Kypers, agent to an international thief from Northern Italy. The latter criminal, it appears, stole from a palace, situated outside the City of Florence, a particular treasure, an artistic Masterpiece, which, when the matter came to Kit Marlowe's ears, filled him with the irresistible desire to possess it above all other things. Fired by his lively imagination, he designed a ruse to obtain the ravishing prize. In due course Kit Marlowe, therefore, careless of all the dreadful risks involved, struck a bargain with the aforesaid Jan de Kypers, secretly, for the purchase of the Masterpiece, aforementioned, which was created out of gold, and duly passed into his hands for this said purpose the number of counterfeit, gold coins, forged by Thomas Williams, as had been contracted, and received in exchange the said Masterpiece. Kit Marlowe then returned to England, where within two months, Thomas Williams, as described, died of the plague.

It was at this time that Kit Marlowe was coming under increasing pressure on account of his most extravagant ways: because of the many and contradictory rumours which continued to circulate about his blaspheming, as some said, and about his Catholic connections, as others claimed; because of the first forgery aforementioned; and also because of his public brawling and duelling, so that ultimately he grew fearful that the authorities could search his lodgings, and come upon the stolen Masterpiece. In these circumstances, wishing to serve the best interests of my Master, I offered to place the Masterpiece in the safest place I know on earth, which is known to no other person outside our Penhalion family – until the situation later on became regularised and it was deemed safe to return the treasure to him."

"…deemed safe to return the treasure…" So the line goes. But what if the golden treasure has already been taken? Suppose somebody discovered the secret of Red Bluff and removed it? Even then there is the possibility that it had been lost in the sea by accident on the way back. Or the adventurer could well have drowned in the attempt – like poor Sydney Sattiscombe. Yet, it could still be waiting for us in the cave.

"As Kit Marlowe regarded me as his true and trusted friend, he well knew that he had no fear in handing over the Masterpiece into my safe-keeping. In due course that is what came to pass. It was at the time of the Autumn Equinox in 1592, when I took out the boat at Red Bluff bay. That was on the occasion – which you must well remember – when I returned to our home from London. I placed the Masterpiece of gold within the metal casket, designed by the goldsmith himself so that it could be safely transported, protected from the rigours of travel. In consequence it fits precisely and once the lid is closed, the box becomes air-tight!"

It all seems to confirm the facts I tracked down during my stay. And it is such a long time ago since I met Mrs. Lescaut at Moorland Farm, when she first told me the Cornish legend. But she only knew about what she laughingly called a "lost cave" – meaning that nobody in modern times knew where it was.

At any rate the letter makes it clear that Kit's Leander placed "the Masterpiece of gold" in the Red Bluff cave – the same cave I believe I saw briefly before the war – through the waves. Let me check Leander's own description of putting the casket in "our family's secret hiding place". Yes, here it is over the page.

"On entering the cave – not without considerable difficulty with the raging seas – I placed the casket into our family's secret hiding place. It was none too soon, perhaps, for (although it was not until the 18th May 1593) the Privy Council was to issue a warrant to Harry Maunder to 'apprehend and bring' Kit Marlowe to the Court on matters relating to charges of heresy and treason.

Meanwhile, as I have discovered, Jan de Kypers – unknown to Kit Marlowe – by coincidence knew an acquaintance of the poet, one Robert Poley, a contact of Thomas Walsingham himself. When therefore, Jan de Kypers, in the course of time, realised that he had been deceived by Kit Marlowe in the matter of the passed, counterfeit coins, he became bitterly enraged and determined to retrieve the Masterpiece. Remembering the said Robert Poley's connection with Kit Marlowe, Jan de Kypers traced and confronted him during one of his frequent visits to Holland. Robert Poley reacted promptly, and with enthusiasm, to the proposals which were put to him. Forthwith and readily therefore he reached agreement with Jan de Kypers that, employing two of his friends to assist in the noxious assignment, Robert Poley was to recover the Masterpiece by the expedient of a festive meeting. The three conspirators, Robert Poley and his two friends, at an appropriate moment were to present Kit Marlowe with evidence of his fraud. If, as expected, he did not comply at once with the demand that he should promptly agree to produce and hand over to them the Masterpiece forthwith, they would instantly set upon the said Kit Marlowe and overcome all his resistance. Then would they with cruel malice restrain him and commence to torture him in order that he should reveal the whereabouts of the Masterpiece.

It fell out therefore that, on Robert Poley's next visit to The Hague at the end of May 1593, he again met Jan de Kypers, who handed over to him specimens of the coins which Kit Marlowe had used in payment for the purchase of the Masterpiece. Armed with this evidence, and also with Jan de Kypers' sworn statement on the matter, that he had been duped and had been passed these coins, together with diverse others of a similar kind, in a fraudulent deal with Kit Marlowe in August 1592, Poley returned to England.

There he went directly, by prior arrangement, to join his two friends, Nicholas Skeres and Ingram Frizer, the latter being a servant to Thomas Walsingham. They all met in Eleanor Bull's tavern at Deptford Strand, where

Was There Ever Seen Such Villainy?

Kit Marlowe had been invited to dinner. After dinner the three men, the said Robert Poley, Nicholas Skeres and Ingram Frizer, turned on Kit Marlow with intent to hold him down and to extract from him by torture a confession relating to the deception, and to enforce him to admit the present whereabouts of the Masterpiece, so that it might be returned to Jan de Kypers. Notwithstanding the suddenness of the ambush and that he was outnumbered, Kit Marlowe resisted with desperate courage, wounding Ingram Frizer by stabbing him twice on the head in the process, but Ingram Frizer was able to stab Kit Marlowe deeply with his own dagger, forcing it back into the skull, at a point over the right eye, from which wound he died instantly. After the event the three plotters stood together by their invented story that it was Kit Marlowe who had suddenly attacked Ingram Frizer in a quarrel over payment of the bill for dinner, and that Ingram Frizer had killed Kit Marlowe in self-defence.

My information comes from a member of the Lord Admiral's Men, whom I shall not name lest this letter should accidentally fall into infamous hands. My informant is a catamite and, in that relationship, knows Robert Poley, who told him, one night in his cups, the truth about all the circumstance pertaining to that terrible evening. The Coroner, William Danby, found, as is recorded, that Frizer killed Kit Marlowe but that he had acted in self-defence."

Harry paused to add a note to his copy of the letter as follows: 'The next pages have been badly damaged. Many words I just can not make out and others are nearly indecipherable, so I have decided, instead of trying to indicate the number of words thought to be missing, I would simply use a single dash to show where a word, or several words, appear to be missing.'

Part 3: Return to Cornwall: September 1946

"I turn next, and in conclusion to the Masterpiece itself and to record precise details – resting place which you, father, have never visited – As you know – hazards present to obstruct any persons intent – Penhalion Cave, which lies at the head of Red Bluff in the small bay at the very – Guardian Tides and the sea's currents – foil the intruder. The key – penetration lies in the knowledge of the Autumn Equinox. The lowest tide will allow but little time within the cave – be warned that a change of wind can ruin any such enterprise."

Now to show Alex the letter, and for a long chat about the possibility of exploring the cave. Leander's description of where the casket lies – plus his warning of the speed of the returning tide are helpful details. So, we'll have to remember that "time and tide wait for no man."

"The cavity, wherein the Masterpiece lies, is sited opposite to the entrance to the cave. It would be nigh impossible to fail to notice the flat-topped stage shaped from a natural ramp of rock lying at the far end. The cavity itself requires a diligent search to trace, one arm's length below the middle point, set inwards beneath the rock platform itself, on which the intrepid seeker must lie, stretched out, face down, in order to feel for and to ease out the casket – which contains the Masterpiece – from the rock, where I have placed it. The Masterpiece, the treasure, is from the hand of the Master Goldsmith, Benvenuto Cellini, the same who created the magnificent and renowned Salt Cellar for the King of France.

But now, I am alone and desolate without my dearest friend, Kit Marlowe, that one who wrote, albeit unconsciously, his own epitaph in that simple line of his greatest poetry:

Was There Ever Seen Such Villainy?

'Cut is the branch that might have grown full straight!'

Guard for me, Father, the Cellini Masterpiece, in memory of the one who meant all the world to your son.
                                        LEANDER PENHALION"

Harry read through the copy letter again. Pleased with the result, he put it in the chest of drawers, but he thought that he should leave the original letter somewhere safer, although not in its first hiding place. He was anxious that the almost invisible join of the layered paper, which concealed the plaster niche, should not become marked by unnecessary movement. Folding the letter exactly as discovered, he looked round the room. Where could he put it? He smiled wryly at himself, conscious of falling into the amateur role of a Sexton Blake type of fictitious detective. But instinct, or a cautious nature, made him search the bedroom until he found a suitable spot. At the back of the deep hanging cupboard, the woodwork had developed corrugations, due perhaps to alternate winter damp and summer sun. He saw that it would be possible to slip the letter between the two open edges of wood, but he did not want to lose it, if it should slip beyond his reach. To overcome the problem, he placed the letter inside his Post Office savings book, which he had brought with him for drawing petty cash. The Post Office book and the letter together were thick enough to lodge securely inside the small opening without being seen from outside the cupboard, as the book fitted into one of the distorted wood curves. He experimented and found that it could be easily retrieved.

Not until that moment did he stop to wonder what the circumstance had been to force Sydney Penhalion, or another hand, to hide his son's letter so completely out of sight – thus resulting in the likely frustration of Leander's compelling plea to his father. But, wandering thoughts would get him no further, and so he began to read through the letter again in the form he had re-set it for a twentieth century reader.

III

Harry stood beside the dwarf wall, gazing across the headland at the blue sea, still and mirroring the sky above. It was already hot. Breakfast over, he had walked through from the house, seeking Alex. He must talk to somebody about the letter and, although he knew he ought to tell the Penhalions in the first place, something held him back. Impatiently he turned and paced up and down on the shingle. Then he heard her voice from the direction of the kitchen.

"Alex!" he called. "When can you be free?"

She emerged, wiping her hands on a small towel.

"Hallo, Harry. I've a full day here, but what's it all about?"

"Well, I wanted to show you something interesting, but I did want a word on our own."

"We can have a talk this evening."

"Can you come to The Ship?"

"Yes, I'm sure Mum can manage then. I'll see you later – I must go."

Harry ran upstairs to fetch binoculars and then hurried down to the beach. As he brushed through the long grass, taking a short cut from the path which joined the cliff top to the shore, his thoughts turned to the night, when he wandered out of the mist and into the light shining from Moorland Farm; eight years was a long time and, after the war years between, it seemed like another world. Yet, Manon's image still lingered in his memory, inflamed by his recent sight of her at The Ship.

Pausing at the cliff edge to look at the sparkling, blue sea below and the stretch of beach, he saw his destination far off, the small, natural quay where he hoped to find Bill Tregoran. Ten minutes later he was standing on the little rock jetty by the cove inlet.

"Is that Harry Guest?" a voice shouted.

Harry saw his old friend with his rolling walk coming toward him. Bill's physical appearance was bulkier and he had grown a beard, very grey, but even after the time lapse his navy blue sweater, with the words 'Sea Queen' across his chest, was exactly as he recalled. The two men shook hands vigorously.

"How's Phil?"

"He's in good form – in the Navy still – in mine-sweepers in the war. I'm afraid he's at sea, but he'll be pleased to hear you're safe."

They exchanged war memories until Harry brought the conversation round to the topic of the sea itself.

"Do you remember when we first met, you laughed at my ignorance of the equinoxes?"

Bill smiled. "No. Did I?"

"Yes, we spoke of the low, autumnal tides at that time, in September. I wonder if the smugglers of old ever had the advantage of local caves which were only uncovered by the Autumn – or Spring – tides? If there was a cave, for example, on a promontory in the sea, it would be possible that the cave could be under water – hidden from view – for most of the year. Such a cave at the time of the equinox could be revealed for a short time, at the lowest tides. Am I right?"

"Oh, yes, of course. In fact I believe there are caves like that in North Cornwall and on the Welsh coast too, rugged rocks battered by the Atlantic. Significantly low tides could reveal a cave which is normally under water. Yes. And also for a period, say a few days, at either time of year."

"And talking of under water caves, I believe the Royal Marine Commandos have used all sorts of sophisticated equipment in their under water operations during raids on the enemy coast."

"Yes, Phil was seconded to them for a while. You just wait and see. They'll develop the same kind of gear as that for sport in the future, and then our little coves will be swamped by people coming down to try out their expensive, new toys."

"That's a long way off – years ahead."

Bill shook his head. "It may be much nearer than you think."

When they parted, Harry returned to the private beach at the Red House Guest House and pushed the dinghy, named Jill, into the sea, where he was soon pulling strongly on the oars. When he came alongside Red Bluff, he found that conditions were ideal for a reconnaissance of the cliff face at the end of the headland. As he rowed under the overhanging rock between the steep pincers, where the clipped end of the Bluff met the sea, he searched for any signs of a change in the shape of the rock at water level, to see if he could detect where the cave could be. His belief in the existence of the cave had been sustained on reading the discovered letter and on matching the brief description in it with his own memory of the elusive sighting before the war. Soon he rested the oars clear of the water, allowing the little boat to drift on the lake-like surface as he raised the binoculars to his eyes for a careful check, as he had so often done on active service. He could see nothing of note. He knew of course that nothing was likely to be visible yet, but he argued that there could be tidal discrepancies and his impatience was pressing. Disappointed, he rowed back and lay down on the sands to soak up the last, hot rays of the sun as the Summer began its slow decline into Autumn.

Eventually the evening arrived. As Harry drove to Lavington, he handed Alex his modernised copy of the letter. He explained that he had left the original in his bedroom as he wanted to avoid damaging it or losing it in the pub. At the same time he told her about the movement of the compressed wallpaper which had revealed the letter's hiding place.

Alex became excited, first of all when she saw the letter's date and subsequently as she read its contents.

"What about that!" she exclaimed. "It confirms the legend." And she added, raising her voice, "It proves that you were right, Harry – all those years ago."

"You mean – the cave?"

"Yes. You did see it before the war, when nobody believed you. And it simplifies our search."

"Let's hope so. Incidentally, Alex, you see that the letter is addressed to Sydney Penhalion from his son, and the writer makes the point that his friend, Kit Marlowe, called him Leander. So, the letter is from Leander Penhalion and it agrees with the legend. It all comes together too with the Autumn Equinox which he mentions. And the next one is just about a week off."

Alex said, "I suppose it would have been on a different date then, because the calendar was altered later. The change must have occurred in this country nearly two hundred years after Leander's visit to the cave. That would have been in the reign of one of the Georges, wouldn't' it?"

"I'd forgotten all about that," Harry said.

"We learned it at school," Alex added. "Pope Gregory suppressed ten days and got the Vernal Equinox to fall on the twenty first of March."

"Gosh, you are up on the subject. Well, the twenty third of September is the Autumn Equinox, which should bring the lowest tides. It's also the day when I saw the cave in 1938. The cave must be under water for most of each year and only shows up on those rare occasions, when the tide is at its lowest ebb. So our best bet is the twenty third. Don't you agree?'

As Harry finished speaking, he drove the car into The Ship's car park, leaped out and ran round to the passenger door to open it for Alex, but she had already climbed out. Together they entered the saloon bar, where two, original, water colour paintings by Birket Forster hung on the wall, pale, pretty shades of country life nearly a century ago.

"What would you like to drink, Alex?"

"Tomato juice, please."

Harry ordered a pint of mild and bitter and brought it with Alex's drink to the table by the window.

"It's pretty empty tonight," she said as he set down the glasses.

He nodded. "Well," he said. "What are we going to do?"

Alex, who was wearing a pink, summer dress printed with pale blue flowers, shook her hair and looked up at him as she answered, "Find the treasure, of course."

"Well, it's not as easy as that. You know what it can be like in the sea beyond Red Bluff. It really depends on the weather."

"And maybe on many other things – like finding the treasure even if we can get inside the cave."

"What I really mean is – what policy should we adopt?"

"Policy?"

"Yes, to start with I'm just an outsider. The letter belongs to your family, so we ought to show it to your father and mother."

He was surprised by her response.

"You make things so difficult, when they don't need to be. Why tell anybody? Surely there's quite simply one safe thing to do: keep it to ourselves. In that way no one else will get to know and there can be no trouble."

Harry said, "You really don't think we should show your parents the sixteenth century letter?"

"No. They won't be able to keep quiet about it. You know what mummy's like. If we agree to keep it to ourselves, we can be sure of an uninterrupted search for the treasure, and if we're successful, that is the time to worry about what to do next."

Harry smiled and lifted his glass and drank.

"Delicious," he said. "It's agreed."

Alex raised her glass as she said, "We keep mum."

"Alex, you called it 'treasure' and the first Leander called it 'a supreme example of the goldsmith's art'. Which means it will be rare and beautiful and gold and very valuable. It also means that in law the object would be regarded as treasure trove. Isn't that so?"

"Are you sure? Why treasure trove if it's part of the Penhalion property?"

"You may be right. We'd have to find out. But it's best if we leave all that till after we've found it – or rather, if we find it! Meanwhile 'there's many a slip 'twixt cup and lip'. It could have been removed and disposed of." He began to count off the possibilities on his fingers. "It could have been lost at sea; trying to bring it ashore or perhaps the person taking it was drowned on the way."

Alex said, "And it could be waiting for us in the cave on the twenty third of September. You're too pessimistic."

"Realistic. But let's hope it's there. This much we know, that a cave regarded as the Penhalions', and guarded by the tides, may hold a treasure of gold."

They had been talking so earnestly that they had altogether forgotten their surroundings, and they had not realised that the neighbouring bar had been occupied. They first became aware that somebody was there, when they heard the sharp scrape of a chair on the floor and a glass knocked over on a table. As they exchanged glances, quick steps sounded and then the door to the public bar opened and closed. Harry strode to the window, but he could not see the adjacent exit, because of the porch, and when he opened the outside door, he could see nobody about.

Disconsolately, he returned to the bar, where he peered at an old, war-time poster which was still fastened to the wall. It was the illustration of a large ear, drawn by the artist so as to create the illusion of standing out in relief; it carried several captions, including "CARELESS WORDS COST LIVES" and "EVEN THE WALLS HAVE EARS". Its original purpose had been to persuade the public to guard their tongues, because German spies, overhearing what was said about troop movements, might pass the information on to the enemy. How ironic, he thought, that they had been so careless, even as they sat beneath the old poster with its cautionary message.

When they returned to the Red House, Jean Penhalion was speaking on the telephone, but she finished her conversation as they were passing in the hall.

"Alex," said her mother, "that was for Leander. Be a dear and write a message on the pad for him to read. It was his friend, Brucey. Apparently Leander rang him a short while ago, when he was out. He spoke to the brother, George, instead. Brucey has just returned and found a note from George to 'phone Leander urgently. The boy was here a short while ago. He can't be far away."

Jean was still speaking when Leander burst in, and so she repeated Brucey's 'phone message to him.

Leander's response was to leave the house as rapidly as he had entered, calling over his shoulder, "O.K., Mum. I've got to go out again. I won't be long."

IV

Lavington had something of a continental feeling about it, the illusion being encouraged by the cobbled, central square with the vast oak tree growing in the middle, reputed to have been planted during the Restoration celebrations. The tree was protected by an aged triangle of wooden posts, each sporting strong rings for tethering horses in by-gone days. Two pubs, The George and The Ship, each had wooden tables and metal chairs outside their premises on the wide pavements, but the square itself was dominated by the Town Hall, an agreeably pretentious building, whose engraved, fulcrum stone, on the archway above the main entrance, bore the inscription 'Built in 1878'. A flight of twelve steps went up to baronial doors, fifteen feet high and painted dark magenta.

It was the custom on every Saturday night of the year to hold a public dance in the Entertainments Room, and tonight's event was in aid of the local Cricket Club. There was a five-piece dance band, consisting of trumpeter, saxophonist, pianist and drummer, which was called The Lavington 5, the fifth member being the band leader, a sturdy white faced man, his black shiny hair fixed in place with Brylcream. His was a versatile role. In addition to conducting the band, he would sing, play the accordion and make all the necessary announcements at the microphone.

It was shortly after 7.30 p.m. and the band was playing; the dancers provided a display of rather muted colours as there was still a large percentage of navy, army and air-force uniforms in evidence; and a few colourful frocks lit up the scene with reds and greens and blues of swirling skirts revealing nylon-stockinged legs. Inside the main entrance at the top of the steps sat an elderly man, a cap covering his white hair. He was dispensing tickets at a green, card table which was occupied by a teddy bear who was being raffled.

Harry led the way past the table, paying for both dance and raffle tickets for the party. Alex, who was just behind him, was dressed in a flimsy, pale yellow frock. She was followed by Vivian with Shrimp who was wearing a red dress with white piping. She was the daughter of the landlord of The Ship where they had picked her up en route. She was less than five feet tall, but she was always the centre of attention, vivacious and witty. They all filed into the dance hall with its 1914-1918 war, upright, wooden chairs on all sides of the room, excepting the stage front which was kept clear. At the far end of the hall, opposite the stage, were a number of varying sized tables. Above, the tall windows were blacked out and also protected by criss-crossing tape against bomb-blast.

The band finished playing a moody waltz time and the band leader announced: "Ladies and Gentlemen, please take your partners for the next dance which will be an Excuse-me foxtrot."

Raising his hands and baton he set the band off at a sprightly beat to the tune of "Kiss me goodnight, sergeant major". Harry asked Shrimp for the dance and they paired off at a pace. Shortly afterwards dancers all over the floor were interrupted as men and women walked on to the floor to tap the shoulder of the partner with whom they wished to dance. Harry was surprised to feel a gentle tap on his shoulder, but as he released Shrimp's hand with a smile, he saw that it was Manon, who was taking over. She grasped him in a professional hold, swinging off amongst the other dancers and, as they moved together, he felt her long legs gliding against his own, until it was, as at their first meeting, that she was pressing hard against him. Out of the corner of his eyes he saw a young man approaching. Manon saw him too. Immediately she said, close to Harry's ear, "Follow me."

They walked swiftly to the outer ring of dancers, Manon leading the way towards the cloakroom.

"It's hot on the floor," she murmured. "It's cooler in the Stalls room."

"Stalls room?" he asked.

"Yes, the Council lease it to traders and it opens out on to the market square on three days a week."

As she spoke she looked about her quickly with a restraining hand resting on his elbow.

Between the "Men" and "Ladies" cloakrooms was a third door, marked "Private: Leaseholders only". A man and two women brushed past them to the separate toilets as they hesitated. Then the corridor was empty and Manon deftly unlocked the central door, pulling Harry after her and closing the door. The room was oblong and illuminated from above by two strip windows, through which filtered the streetlights from outside. Manon was dressed in a long, black gown held together at the waist by a black cloth belt which was partly sewn on to the soft, woollen material. From the high collar, turned up to frame her head and dark hair, the lapels dipped to a point just above the belt, so that her slim throat showed to effect the white pearls which she wore above the curve of barely concealed breasts. In the half light Harry could see her white skin, the beautiful, oval face and plump cheeks, the large, dark eyes and full mouth, but that was all, the black dress camouflaged her body as she stood against the dingy interior of the Stalls room.

"I've waited too long for this moment," she whispered.

Harry could feel his heart racing.

"You are beautiful!" he said.

Suddenly she made a quick movement with both hands at her dress belt, and then she was naked but for the pearls at her throat and the high heeled, black satin shoes on her feet. As she dropped the gown to the floor, he noted that she had no underwear beneath the dress. He stared at the pear-shaped breasts trembling with her rapid breathing.

"Manon!" Harry cried. "Yes, it's been too long."

Then they held each other close as the subdued sound of the band drifted through from the hall.

It was at this unpropitious moment that the door behind Harry's back burst open and struck the rear wall with a crash.

"Whoops!" said a loud feminine voice. "Sorreeey!"

He recognised Shrimp, and Vivian, who was with her, said, "Sorry, old boy. On the job?"

Behind the couple other faces were beginning to appear and Harry tried to cover Manon, as she hurriedly retrieved her dress, quickly pulling it round her and clipping the belt in place. Harry slammed the door shut and grasped Manon to him but for the moment the magic had gone.

"No," she said. "Not now."

Some minutes later Vivian had a broad smile on his face as Harry came up to the long table, where he was now seated with a giggling Shrimp.

"Harry, old chap," said Vivian. "I'll get you some beer so you can cool down. But first of all come and meet our neighbours. Did you in fact meet Maurice Lescaut, Manon's brother, before the War?"

Part 3: Return to Cornwall: September 1946

Maurice's dark, gipsy-like face was wreathed in a friendly smile. "Oh, yes, we met alright – when I pulled you out of the ditch."

He shook Harry's hand firmly as Manon pushed sideways along the table and sat next to Leander.

Vivian continued, "And opposite Leander is Captain Bruce-Parkinson, but he says we are to call him Brucey. That's right, isn't it, Brucey?"

Harry's eyes held those of the tall newcomer, whom he judged must be at least ten years older than the rest of the party, and, as he stared, he had the feeling that – somewhere, at some time during the war – they had met before, although he could recall neither the place nor the occasion.

"Good evening," he said. "Haven't we met?"

Parkinson hesitated before shaking his head. "No. I don't think so."

Harry thought that the words were slurred, as if the man had been drinking heavily.

Leander then spoke. "Brucey's a very old friend of mine. He's an expert on antiques and books. His family have an antiquarian shop in Soho."

Vivian was moving to buy a round of drinks, but Harry pushed him back, winking and saying, "This is on me – and you keep quiet." He put mock emphasis on the last words.

Meanwhile Alex was talking to Maurice and laughing.

Harry took the order and returned to the table some twenty minutes later, carrying a tin tray, heavy with spilling pints of beer and glasses of gin plus separate, opened bottles of tonic water and an orange squash for Alex. As he set the tray down at the end of the table, he realised even above the gay music of the band and the loud chatter from all sides, that the atmosphere had changed during his long wait at the crowded bar.

Manon was saying, angrily, "What is the matter with you, Brucey? Can't I talk to Leander without you getting

87

so up-tight? Leander has worked with Maurice at our farm throughout the war, as you know. Our families have all been friends for years. Don't be so possessive."

"Don't you talk to me like that, young woman," said Parkinson.

Leander was anxious. "Brucey, please," he appealed.

"Oh, be your age. You're old enough to know better!" Manon persisted.

"Shut up, you bitch!" yelled Brucey, cheeks crimson, eyes glazed with drink, and he brought his fist down sharply on to the table so that a number of the glasses spilled. The tonic water bottle, standing in front of Manon's glass of gin, which she had not yet mixed, flew into the air and fell in her lap, soaking her dress.

She leaped to her feet and flung the gin from her glass into Parkinson's face.

Harry said, "Cool it now. Behave yourself, Brucey."

The words galvanised Parkinson, who stood up and lunged across the table at Harry. Vivian and Maurice jumped up and seized Parkinson's arms as Vivian called to Harry, "Take Alex for a dance."

The evening had been ruined. By the time Harry returned to the table, Maurice had left, taking Manon back to the farm and dropping Leander off at the Red House. Meanwhile Parkinson had been left to walk on his own to the Kemp-Reydon Guest House, where he was staying, on the outskirts of Lavington.

Yet despite everything the dance concluded with a cheerful result, when the band leader called out the number of Alex's raffle-draw ticket. She went to the platform, her red hair about her white shoulders, to receive the teddy bear which she had won.

V

The day broke to an eerie stillness. There was everywhere a heavy sea mist. Harry was late getting up. He felt sluggish and dissatisfied with himself, ruffled by the events at the Lavington dance the night before. When he reached the dining room eventually, the rest of the household had already breakfasted, but Alex brought him a plateful of hot food and a jug of coffee. She sat on the chair opposite, holding a mug of coffee between her hands. Outside, the mist hung about near the windows. The other Penhalions seemed to have departed as there were no sounds either from the kitchen or elsewhere in the house. It was very quiet.

Alex was wearing a blue gingham dress with a green cardigan which complemented her red hair, well brushed and shining in the artificial light from the lamp over the table. Harry looked up at her pretty face with the pale, freckled skin. He gave her a sour smile.

"What an evening!"

"That man! What a horror he is! Mummy and Daddy can't stand him. Leander and Brucey have been friends – if that's what you call it – for years now and there's nothing they can do about it. It's as if Brucey – ugh, what a ridiculous name! – had some sort of hold over my brother. Leander's fixed by him like a rabbit by a stoat."

"There's quite a difference in age, too, isn't there?"

"Yes, ten years. Leander admires the man. And of course, he does have a grasp of his trade, and he comes from a tough cosmopolitan background which appeals to Leander. I think he is fascinated by the idea of Soho, antiques, the book trade and the rough-and-tumble of back street London, in contrast to Cornwall. This!" She nodded to the misty silence beyond the closed windows.

"It's a strange parallel, isn't it?" Harry asked. "That is – with this sixteenth century namesake, who was also fascinated by London. It must have been an even greater contrast in those days between the London of the Lord Admiral's Players and the Cornwall of smugglers, Customs men, dragoons and fishermen!"

"You're right. But, the first Leander must have been stronger intellectually – especially after what we know from his letter, and not just the picture. He must have been bright to have attracted Kit Marlowe and to have gained his complete trust. I'm afraid our Leander's not like that."

She hesitated before going on, "Harry, can I say this, just to you?"

Harry glanced at her quickly. "Yes, of course. You mean in confidence?"

"Yes. Yes, about Leander. He's been a terrible worry to my poor parents. It's that he's so completely wilful and irresponsible. He doesn't seem to think or care about anyone but himself. He's always been like that from a little boy. Honestly I think there's something missing there." She shook her head. "For example, he was always in trouble and one day, when he and some friends smashed a window in the Post Office in Lavington, the other boys all ran off but Leander stayed behind, unmoving on the pavement, until the Postmistress ran out and seized him and got in touch with Daddy."

"Almost like a cry for attention or help, poor chap."

"Yes, I suppose so. And at boarding school later on, he was expelled after being caught stealing money and, during the same term he was found in bed with a younger boy."

"I see." Harry smiled encouragingly as she looked so miserable. "Viv told me he was ambidextrous."

She laughed. "He would. But it's all very well. Look where it's got him – with Brucey for nine years. And Brucey gets so jealous and possessive, as you saw last night. I think he's dangerous. Do you know what? I wouldn't be surprised if Brucey had been inside."

"Done time? Could be. His gaunt thinness is like Cassius – in *Julius Caesar* with the *'lean and hungry look'*," he said. "You remember – *'such men are dangerous'*?"

"Do you really think so?"

"I'm very serious."

"I hope we're wrong. But what do you make of our Leander?"

Harry frowned. "I've not actually thought about it. He's not like the rest of the family, a little bit glum. Is he moody?"

"Yes. And he can't help being conceited, he's so good looking. But he's alright – he can be a very nice boy, too."

"Good." Harry smiled. "But, about Brucey, I've been thinking. When I first saw him, I had the distinct impression we'd met before. And I've suddenly got it. It was at the end of the war. We were in Germany and there was a court martial. The facts don't matter except that one of the witnesses cracked under cross-questioning at the trial. The man who cracked was Brucey. His evidence wasn't reliable, but what is more interesting is this: he was not Captain Geoffrey Bruce-Parkinson then; his name and rank was Corporal Bruce Parkinson. What about that?"

"You mean he's an impostor?"

"Not really. Just a vain, stupid man who's given himself a false rank and grander-sounding name. But he's not to

91

be underestimated. I'm sorry for your parents though, that Leander has made him such a close friend – and last night's display of drunken, bad temper caps it all. Try not to worry. You can't change the unchangeable."

Alex stood up. "That's true. Well, if you've finished, I'll take your things, Harry. I'm afraid you've a rather wasted day with the mist. It will be with us all day."

Depressed Harry walked into the mist outside and down the hill path towards the coves below. He had no particular plan, but he wanted time to think. He could not, however, get his thoughts of Manon out of his mind.

Ridiculous, but I can't help a feeling of guilt about Alex, when I think of Manon. Yet she's quite different. She's my friend. And anyhow I must get on and make sure I have everything ready for an attempt on the cave. Leander's letter puts the date clearly with the Autumn Equinox. So the cave comes into view, uncovered by the lowest tides on the calendar. Not surprising it's been lost for so long. The cave is "at the head of Red Bluff", according to the letter. Right, I will borrow one of the dinghies, Jack or Jill, and row out there. Will try to land and pull the boat out of view. Leander leaves no doubt about how little time there is to search inside. But first of all I must be able to see – a good torch for the dark interior. And after hundreds of years being wedged in the rocks, the casket may not come away easily. I shall see what I can find at the ironmonger, perhaps at St. Aubyn, a jemmy or something like it.

Then the casket itself – just as well Leander is so exact. I have to feel for a cavity, lying flat on my face, around the middle of the rock platform which he describes. And, with luck, the casket will be in my hand. But, the casket will need to be protected. I must keep it safely on me. A sturdy satchel with a strong shoulder strap is what's wanted. Must not let the casket drop in the sea! And if the boat capsizes, the casket must at all costs stay with me!

Part 3: Return to Cornwall: September 1946

The whole plan depends on some kind of alarm system in case anything unexpected miscarries. There has to be an agreed time with Alex when she must go for help, if I fail to return. I did suggest taking Vivian into our confidence, but she said, "No. Wait until we're home and dry, when we can let all the family in on the secret." I couldn't do anything but agree.

At this stage of his contemplative walk, Harry realised that he could hear the sound of waves breaking with a gentle splash on the shore. At first he thought that the sound was rising to him on the heights as, deep in thought, he had taken no account as to whether he was walking up or down hill, but the sound was close and he felt the change of surface under foot as he stepped from turf onto the sand of the beach. Keeping the noise of the continuous slap of water to his right, he walked along to his left, intending to mount to the top of Red Bluff before returning to the Red House, where he hoped for some more, hot coffee. He climbed from the sand back to the grass and moved at a faster pace uphill, until the churning sea echoed far below. Shortly after, the ground levelled out and he stood on the Bluff, breathing in the damp air.

As he paused, he heard an unexpected murmur of voices and a rustling of grass indicating that there were others out walking in the mist too. Harry put his head to one side and opened his mouth, an automatic reflex from night patrolling in the war; it was supposed to help the ear to pick up sounds in the dark. There it was again. It must be from behind a shoulder of land, possibly on one of the paths. If he followed the direction of the voices, he would probably come across the path at the same time. It struck him as extraordinary that anybody else should be out in a thick mist on the Bluff heights at this time of day. After three minutes his feet came upon the path and he could hear the voices more clearly. There seemed to be two men. Then he saw their shapes and he stopped. One man was tall and thin and his companion was shorter. Each was wearing a duffle coat with the hood up, which made identification even more difficult. Yet, as Harry stood still, he knew who the taller man was, not only from the boom of his voice but also from his tiresomely repeated use of the word 'laddy'; it was the voluble Parkinson. He was saying, "Risks are always worth taking. It doesn't matter if we put a lot of effort into it and nothing comes of our efforts. If we don't put effort into it, laddy, we're not going to get what we want. And one thing stands out like a lighthouse, the rewards at the far end of our journey could be fabulous."

Harry heard the other voice but could not make out the words spoken. He thought it was Leander.

Parkinson replied, "Well, we've heard that it's gold. I've contacts for the disposal of gold and art treasures on the American market, highly lucrative."

Harry was puzzled. The shapes in front of him started to move towards him, so he subsided slowly into the grass and slithered sideways out of view and away from the path.

As the couple passed nearby, he heard Parkinson say, "Yours is a watching game and we must keep in close touch. Give me a tinkle at once if you come across anything more interesting. You see…"

But that was all. Harry waited for ten minutes, to be sure that the pair had time to get off the Bluff, before he cautiously walked back to the Red House. Parkinson's words bothered him. He had talked of gold and art treasures and the lucrative American market; and what could he have meant by saying that his companion's game was a watching one? As he thought about it, an uneasy feeling came over him. Could the conversation have referred to the Penhalion treasure? Was he letting his imagination run wild? Surely his talk with Alex that night at The Ship had not been overheard? But he recalled that at the time he had thought that they had been careless. And he remembered the glass knocked over and the door closed sharply as somebody left the public bar in a hurry. Yet he half-dismissed the idea, saying to himself, "I've been reading too many thrillers."

At the Red House Harry had coffee and afterwards started his car and drove off northward at 15 m.p.h. with dipped headlights, as the mist was still thick. Some minutes later he noticed that visibility was improving but, when he tested the headlamp beams, the lights reflecting on the mist dazzled him, and he continued with dipped lights until he drove into Moorland Farm, where he pulled up, climbed out and knocked on the door. As there was no reply, he walked round the outhouses at the back of the farm, where he found Maurice by the stables.

"Hello," said Harry. "I wanted to thank you for helping Viv with that looney, Brucey, at the dance last night."

"Oh, it's Harry. That's alright. What a sod the man is. I can't understand young Leander. They're as close as clams."

"It's a pity. I agree. But is Manon about?"

"No. She went off early. I don't know where. And Leander's late this morning, very unusual. I don't know what's up with him. Held up by the mist, I expect."

As he spoke, they heard the sound of a car's engine labouring in low gear, and then they saw gleaming, diffused lights shining though the mist, heralding the car's arrival. It was Leander, who parked the car by the stables and came over.

"Morning, Maurice," he said, ignoring Harry. "Sorry I'm late. I've been held up by the mist."

Harry climbed into his car and waved and he started the engine. Pulling out on to the main road, he thought to himself, it was not just the mist which delayed Leander. Look what I've done in the time – got up late, walked on Red Bluff, driven out here after coffee – and I've still reached the farm ahead of him. And Maurice said it was unusual for him to be late. I am sure that he was with Parkinson on the

Bluff, and then he must have taken Parkinson to catch the London train from St. Aubyn. That's what delayed him as well as the mist.

VI

H arry decided that the mist was not going to clear, but he was determined to try to get to Plymouth as he was anxious to call at the public library there to see what information he could find about Christopher Marlowe. The local legend intrigued him and he wanted to know more. To reach the city he would have to pass through St. Aubyn, and if the mist was too thick by the time he got there, he could check at the station to see how the trains were running. When he arrived, he parked in the station car park. The booking clerk reported that the train services had been delayed generally by about ten minutes and that the next Plymouth train was due in twenty minutes.

He realised, after his uncomfortable drive over the moors that it was not worth continuing in the car, so he bought a return ticket to Plymouth. The booking clerk showed him where the Council Offices were situated, close to the station and visible in the mist as a blaze of light from its many windows. He went over and picked up a copy of the South West Coast Tide Tables

His train was later than estimated and so on arrival at Plymouth he hired a taxi to the City library. His search was at first disappointing. There seemed to be little about Marlowe, only an introduction to his plays, which included

97

brief details of the playwright's life and tragic death in a tavern brawl at Deptford in 1593, when he was under thirty years of age. But later the librarian showed him what he described as the classic biography which had been published during the war. It was by Frederick Boas who had studied his subject for most of his life. At last there was much for Harry to note as he turned the pages of the book enthusiastically.

Later, Harry took down several hefty books from the Art History section to see what more he could find about the artist, Cellini. He remembered the goldsmith's name simply because of his wild reputation, recalling that he had actually confessed to murder. The first Leander's letter described how he had taken the masterpiece, which he called a "supreme example of the goldsmith's art" and concealed it inside a cave near his home in Cornwall. He was therefore anxious to discover more details concerning the masterpiece itself. Thumbing through the library's Dictionary of Art, he came to the entry under "Cellini – Benvenuto – 1500-1571: born in Florence: trained in Rome, 1519: travelled to France, 1540: worked in Florence, 1545-1571." So, according to those dates, Marlowe was about to enter the world's artistic stage as Cellini departed. The Dictionary suggested that, apart from Cellini's remarkable autobiography, first printed in 1558, his claim to fame as an artist had rested on four outstanding works: the bronze figure of Perseus, with the outstandingly beautiful figurines and reliefs incorporated on the pedestal of the statue; the famous salt cellar which he created in gold, including magnificent enamelling, for the King of France, Francis I (and which is the sole remaining example of his goldsmith's craft); the Nymph of Fontainebleau, a vast relief, made also for the King but in bronze; and a crucifix which Cellini described in his book as "one of the most difficult things in the world. It is a Christ of whitest marble on a cross of blackest marble, of the size of a well-grown man". Unfortunately there was only one illustration, a colour photograph of the beautiful and sensual saltcellar of Francis I.

Harry stayed at the library for several hours taking notes. As he travelled back, he wondered at the extraordinary time of the Renaissance. After struggling out of the dark ages and from medieval centuries, the western world had blossomed into the breathtaking light of a time and scale of creation which verged on the miraculous. One of his intriguing notes fascinated him: Cellini had referred to a kind of club in Florence, where Leonardo da Vinci, Michelangelo and many other famous artists of the day would meet. What an amazing gathering it must have been! In his imagination, however, his thoughts strayed home to Elizabethan England and to Shakespeare and so to Marlowe. He felt so close to Kit Marlowe after reading the Leander letter. And the treasure? He had no illusions about that and about the cave, but it seemed to him unlikely that he would ever hold a Cellini object in his hand; and yet he had to suppress a growing feeling of excitement even at such a remote prospect.

When he got back to the Red House, he went upstairs. There was no running hot and cold water in the bedroom, although both were laid on to the bathroom at the end of the corridor, where he washed. On returning he brushed his hair and sat down on the wooden chair in front of the dressing table.

For security, and also for easy reference, he had left his copy of Leander's letter beneath his clean underwear in the chest of drawers, thinking that this was an unlikely place for it to be found. But, when he pulled out the drawer, he was shocked to see that the contents had been turned upside down. Worst of all there seemed to be only two sheets of the copy letter remaining. Appalled he picked up the two pages. Thank Heavens, they were the vital part of the letter, specifying exactly where the casket had been placed within the cave. Without that information anyone wanting to discover the treasure would be handicapped.

His feelings of relief were, however, changed by a frantic thought: what about the original letter? He had concealed it behind the wardrobe, inside his Post Office book. Kneeling by the wardrobe, he opened the door and carefully eased the hidden book from the split wood, where it had been forced. As he took the original letter from the pages, he let out a gasp of relief. Whoever had been in his bedroom had failed to discover it. But, most of the copied pages had been taken – stolen. Enough details on paper to whet any thief's appetite.

Dinner at the Red House was late that evening as Jean was waiting for Leander. However, when the grandfather clock struck eight o'clock, she decided to bring in the meal, leaving a portion in the oven for her son's return.

Meanwhile six of them sat round the oval table. As it was nearing the end of the season, there were no other guests present in the dining room. Dan sat at the head of the table distributing portions from an outsize dish full of shepherd's pie: Jean was next to him; Alex and Harry were seated opposite each other; Vivian, who was on the other side of his father, was busily pouring out drinks from one of the flagons of beer, which he had brought from The Ship; by his side was Shrimp, talking non-stop; and Leander's empty place was beside Alex. As the family came together, there was an immediate buzz of conversation which almost overwhelmed Shrimp's words. Despite the dampening effect of the persistent mist outside, the company was in a good mood until half way through the meal when Leander returned, slamming the outside door behind him as he entered the house.

"Are you alright, Leander?" called his mother. When he failed to answer, Jean got up.

Dan grumbled, "Your food will get cold."

"I must see if he's alright and get his plate out of the oven. It won't take a second."

Some minutes later Leander appeared, looking cross, and sat down next to his sister without saying a word. Meanwhile the universal chatter continued undiminished as his mother returned.

Jean raised her voice to ask brightly, "How did you get on at the dance last night? Alex tells me that your friend, Brucey, was there, Leander, and he made a scene."

"He was plastered," explained Vivian.

"That was no excuse for the way he treated Manon," said Harry.

"What happened?" asked Dan.

Vivian described how they had had to restrain Parkinson when he had become belligerent.

"How very unpleasant!" said Jean.

Leander was angry. "They were all against Brucey," he said.

"Rubbish!" cried Shrimp. "He's a nasty old man. What do you see in him, Leander?"

Leander answered fervently, "You don't understand him. He's very clever, you know. And last night he was provoked and we'd all been drinking."

"Provoked, my foot!" said Vivian in his forthright way. "What do you say, Harry?"

The room became quiet as everybody waited to hear Harry's reply. It was to have incalculable consequences.

Harry looked across the table at Leander and said, "Drink or not there was no excuse for his being so quarrelsome – and brawling – he was out of control. And he spoiled our jolly evening."

Leander glared furiously at him.

Harry finished by saying, "You want to know what I think, Vivian? I think the man's a bad-tempered old poofter."

Was There Ever Seen Such Villainy?

There was complete silence now. Leander's face was white. He stood up, scraping the chair noisily on the floor.

"You'll be sorry for that!" was all he said as he strode out of the room, leaving his half-consumed meal behind.

"Leander -" Dan began to say, sharply, but his son ignored him and ran upstairs to his bedroom.

"Oh dear!" exclaimed Jean. "He's so bound up with that man. But you were a bit strong, Harry."

"On the contrary, Mum. It was true and just as well it was said," Vivian replied with feeling. "Anyway, let's forget about it. There's nothing more to be done."

"I'm sorry, Jean. I shouldn't have said that, but we were having such fun at the dance before Brucey ruined the night out."

Shrimp laughed hysterically as she remembered the scene in the Stall's room.

"You did have fun, Harry," she managed to say.

Vivian at once announced firmly, "Enough! And now, more drinks, anybody?"

VII

Next day at breakfast Jean was about to leave the table as Harry entered the room.

"Good morning, Harry," she said. "I wanted to see you."

"Good morning, Jean. What a super morning it is! And what can I do?"

"Nothing much. I just have to ask if you would mind moving your things from your bedroom – along to number six, at the far end of the house. It will only be for a couple of nights. I hope not more."

"Of course, what's happening?"

"We had a noisy storm a month or so ago which damaged the window in your room. We tried to get the repair done by our nice Mr. Rowse from the next village, but he wasn't free until now. He's called to say he'll be in to do the job in the next day or so."

"I never noticed the damage."

"It's not all that serious, but the main window frame has to be re-set. We have to get it put right before the next storm. Our Mr. Rowse thinks the whole window could be sucked out in a heavy gale."

"Fine by me, Jean. I'll go and sort it out as soon as I've finished here."

After breakfast, and having changed his bedroom upstairs, he went outside where Alex was waiting for him. They had arranged to walk on the cliffs.

Alex led the way East of Red Bluff down the cliff path, where it wound high above Eastern Cove. Yesterday's mist had vanished; instead a warm sun lit the bright day from the blue sky where puffs of white cloud raced past on a strong West wind which also flattened the long grass. Southwards stretched the royal blue sea glinting silver and white as the wind disturbed its surface. Along the hillside, dipping to the cliff edge, grew a spectacular display of slender mullein whose tall stems, decked out in rounded, yellow-faced flowers, backed by long green, crinkly leaves, peeped above the grass at waist height.

Alex's white skirt was pressed against her legs by the wind as she walked up the incline, where the path led to a plateau of ground which followed the line of the shore. She wore a dark, blue shirt and on her feet white, canvas shoes. She glanced up at Harry striding at her side. He had just told her about the stolen letter.

"Who would do such a thing? Who could know the letter existed? Who would want it? I think it's awful. Why?"

Harry said, "I haven't told you about my morning stroll, when I left you yesterday after breakfast. I wanted to think things over, even though the mist was so thick. But the mist is the curious part of the story. It was odd enough I should think of going out for a walk on Red Bluff in those conditions. You really couldn't see more than a few yards in front of you, not sensible with the sheer drop to the sea nearby. Anyhow I persisted and the silence on the moist headland, with the soothing splash of the surf below, was what I wanted. But after a while I heard voices, and one of them I recognized at once. It was Brucey. I could hear snatches of words but nothing at all of what his companion said – nor did I see him so as to identify him. But Brucey kept repeating that absurd "laddy" which I've only ever heard used by him. He mentioned the need to put a lot of effort into something that could be fabulous. He said he had contacts for the disposal of gold and art treasures on the American markets. He ended by saying that the whole business could be 'highly lucrative'".

"And you didn't hear a single word of what the other person was saying?"

"No. Brucey ended by telling his colleague that his task was a 'watching game' and to give him 'a tinkle' if he 'came across anything more interesting'. I let them return and, as I was walking back to the Red House to fetch my car, I remembered the evening at The Ship when we were together and thought that the other bar was empty. We talked about the Leander letter which I'd just found. It's easy to say so now, but I realised how obvious it was that we should have been more careful – and taken notice of the war-time poster - 'Even The Walls Have Ears'. We were silly. Somebody must have overheard our conversation and passed the details on to Brucey. And Brucey's visit to Cornwall came after the conversation, so it is possible he travelled from London as soon as he was told about our talk. Art dealer, crooked most likely, and with the means of disposing of a uniquely valuable art treasure, it all fits him. I never saw who he was with."

Alex said, "But you know as well as I do, who it was, don't you? I mean, who was on the Bluff and who stole the copy letter?"

"I suppose you mean Leander?"

"Of course. Who else could it be?"

"It could be somebody else. And I suppose there could be a quite innocent explanation for the missing letter. One of the girls at the Red House might have thought that the copy letter was waste paper and cleared it up."

"What – under your clothes in the chest of drawers?"

"No. I was thinking that I might have carelessly left the letter out – although I don't believe I did."

"Of course you didn't. You would have been very careful."

"As careful as we were in The Ship?"

He saw that she was hurt by the sarcasm in his voice, and so he stopped and held both her hands.

"Sorry, Alex," he said. "I'm cross with myself, not with you. I chose the pub for our talk and I thought all was well, when we found the saloon bar empty."

Alex looked away as she said, "But, it comes down to this: Leander is the only person who is likely to have been with Brucey on the Bluff."

"You're right. And there's something else I haven't told you. I called at Moorland Farm after my walk. I was chatting to Maurice, when Leander drove up, very late for work. He said that he had been delayed by the mist."

Harry thought that he detected a change in her expression, but the wind was blowing the hair about her face so that he could not be sure.

Damn, he said to himself, I hadn't meant to let her know that I went to find Manon – but she doesn't know that. I'm imaging things.

Alex said sharply, "The boy's always been the same. It's typical of him."

Harry made no comment, but he asked, "What's their next move then?"

"They will want to get to the cave," she replied. "But they don't know where it is, so, they'll have to follow us, won't they?"

"And do you assume that they will know the date of the Autumn Equinox?"

"Oh, yes."

"But even if they know the date is the twenty third of September", Harry said, "there may be several tides, when the cave would be uncovered – and perhaps the tides would be at their lowest on more than one day. In that case, they'd have to keep a pretty close watch on us. Otherwise they could miss the hour when we actually arrived there. That's how they'll be thinking, I'm sure. The timing is going to be crucial for us both. It is all poised on the tide – when the tide turns. The cave's not going to be on view for long, you know. Whenever we get there, the tide will all too rapidly return to hide the cave from prying eyes for another equinox or another tide or two at the most. We're assuming a lot. The letter actually gives no dates. Leander merely writes that he entered the cave at the time of the Autumn Equinox."

They had reached the plateau and were leaning into the wind as the path turned, for a brief section of its length, to within a few feet of the edge of the cliff.

Alex said, "Let's sit here for a minute."

They sat together, the colourful country rising to the ridge behind their backs, the headland to their right, the wide sweep of Eastern Cove to their left and the incessant movement of the sea below, breaking on the shore.

Alex tapped Harry's outstretched leg.

"Listen," she said. "You know what I'm getting at. There could be a dispute – to give the least painful calculation of what could happen. And if Brucey was there, do you think it would be a painless confrontation?"

"It could be disagreeable, but there would be no reason for it to be painful – unless the treasure trove had been discovered by one or other side. If neither side knows exactly where it is, there's nothing to get uptight about, is there? And if Leander was involved, less likely still, wouldn't you think? It then becomes a family affair, surely?"

"It's a family affair already, and if Leander's involved – and I think he is – then why hasn't he spoken to me or to my parents?"

"Because he's not going to. Because he can't. Because Leander will do anything that Brucey tells him to. That's what I think. However that may be, the essence of the whole issue is that nobody – as far as we know – has any idea where the casket can be found inside the cave; and you don't suppose after some four hundred years safekeeping the cave is going to yield up its treasure so easily, without a searcher having the exact details, which the last pages of the letter set out so clearly?"

"No. We may miss it this year, but there will not be a next year. Suppose they decide – at whatever time of year – to go into the cave using modern, underwater equipment? If they did, time and tide would matter less. They could even choose the best weather conditions. In addition, without the tide to bother with so much, they could take as long as necessary to find the casket, couldn't they?"

"Alex, of course you're right. What good thinking. But, you're wrong in saying 'we'. It's a case of 'I'. You can't possibly come. In the first place you can't be free. You've got those friends of your family, the Simpsons, coming all day and you'll be needed at home. You will be the safeguard. You will know, when we estimate that I should be back after the tide turns, and when to raise the alarm if I'm late."

"No, Harry!"

"Alex, we don't want to draw attention to our plans, do we? You'll be in at the kill if I get the casket, because we'll open it together. It's the opening up that's going to be the fun of it. We're agreed that, if possible, we don't want to involve the rest of the family, and if Leander's in the know, I believe our diagnosis is correct and he won't be telling anybody anything, except Brucey."

"I don't like it."

"Nor do I. I would much prefer you to come along, but there's no point in more than one of us facing the few risks there are: the sea is always treacherous off Red Bluff point; the weather could change suddenly; and I'm not rowing out if the weather's bad; then there's the submerged rocks and the difficulty of rowing into and out of the mouth of the cave with the sort of seas that splash against the headland, even on the best of days."

Alex, to Harry's surprise, spoke tartly. "I suppose you're as safe as houses – a charmed life. Thank God you survived the War, but that's no reason to risk your life on a silly venture now."

Neither of them spoke for a minute. At last Harry said, "I'm not taking anything for granted. I'm not suggesting that I take any unnecessary risks – for example I would wear one of the Red House guests' life-jackets – whatever the weather. I've rowed out there before, as I told you, and so I know what it's like. I'm fit too, so I should be able to cope. Honestly, there shouldn't be any foolish risks to be taken. It ought to be straightforward."

Alex smiled, but she repeated, "I don't like it," and added, "I do like the life-jacket plan."

Harry said, "I know that you would like to go to the cave, Alex, but it would really be more difficult for two of us. We would each worry about the other. It seems to me that it's a job for one of us only. And the issue itself is clear cut: the problems are getting into and then out of the cave and, of course, finding the casket, and the main worry is the unknown – that is to say, how much time the tide's going to allow inside the cave. Look at it this way. It's just a holiday game with elusively high stakes, plus the question mark regarding what the other side may do, Brucey that is – pure 'Boys Own Paper' stuff."

Alex put out her hand as Harry got to his feet. He pulled her up after him.

"What do you say?" he asked.

"We'll see!" said Alex.

VIII

"You've really got something here, laddy. This is some find you've brought."

It was Parkinson speaking. Sitting in the backroom of the shop in Soho, established over one hundred years ago in an early Georgian property, he was hunched beneath a simple, Chinese-hat style electric lamp, green shade on the outside and faded white inside, casting a well-defined light directly on to a dark, green Victorian table cloth with heavy, decorative bobbles at its extremities. There were six mahogany, round-back chairs drawn up to the table and two of them, nearest to a small, coal fire were occupied: Parkinson, as he examined a letter, was speaking to Leander.

"Have they noticed the loss of the letter yet?"

Leander moved uncomfortably in his chair before answering, "I don't know. I 'phoned you as soon as I got my hands on it. Cheek! It's the family property. Just like my sister. Anyway there's nothing to involve me, so we're O.K. And I've told them that I've come to London, because you need help as your brother had to be away." He paused before going on. "But if that masterpiece in the cave is as special as my namesake suggests, then we'll have to work together, Brucey."

110

"I'll do everything for you, laddy. Leave it to me. But we've a long way to go yet."

Parkinson and Leander had been friends for years. Their initial meeting in Soho before the war had been a matter of pure chance. On the day in question, Leander had been a member of a party of boys on an educational trip, organised by his school to visit King's College Chapel and later to see Molière's *Le Malade Imaginaire* at the Arts Theatre in Cambridge and on the next day to attend the National Gallery and afterwards to go on to St. Paul's Cathedral before returning to Cornwall. Leander had managed to give his party the slip on the second day, between the programmed visit to the National Gallery and the Cathedral, getting back to mingle with the party again as it was preparing to move on to St. Paul's. He had walked shiftily away from the school group outside the Gallery in Trafalgar Square and into the seedy backstreets of Soho, where he had wandered into the Antiques-cum-Antiquarian Bookshop, a unique combination in the area, owned by Charles Parkinson who at the time had employed his two sons, George and Geoffrey, to assist him. George, the elder brother, had run the antiques side of the business while Geoffrey had handled the book trade. When Charles died during the war, George had taken over the firm while Geoffrey had been called up to serve in the army; in view of his age, at the time twenty eight years, and his literary background, Geoffrey had been transferred, after his basic training, into the Intelligence Corps with the rank of Corporal. It had been in that unit that Geoffrey had first become known as Brucey, taken from his second Christian name, Bruce.

When Parkinson had met Leander, he had at once been attracted by the youth's enthusiastic interest in the shop's contents. He had also noted Leander's girlish looks and manner, and had promptly invited him to have tea and cakes in the backroom, where he had questioned the boy thoroughly about his home and background.

Young Leander had been fascinated by the close attention which Parkinson had lavished on him and by Parkinson himself, his deep, baritone voice, his mannered style and his clothes which, for the times, had been outlandishly colourful: purple cord jacket, dark blue trousers, pink shirt with pale blue bow tie and all set off with blue, suede shoes. Leander had, in fact, instantly taken to what he had seen as a romantic dream-world of books and antiques and paintings, and he had talked freely, as he had never talked either at home or at his school in Cornwall. Whenever he had stopped chattering, he had listened intently to the literary and antiquarian stories which had flowed from Parkinson's lips. The two had become close friends despite the disparity in their ages; and the long years of the war, with all the travel and other restrictions, had not prevented them from keeping in frequent touch with each other. It had developed into a friendship which Dan and Jean had found both puzzling and a cause for anxiety, but they had not seen enough of Parkinson, as he called himself in those days, to be alarmed; and the man had the appearance of being both erudite and entertaining, even if his "laddys" and his "dear boys" in conversation had begun to pall after a while.

After the war, when Parkinson returned to Civvy Street, he was known as Captain Geoffrey Bruce-Parkinson. Vivian's view of his brother's friend was that he was "a bloody, old phoney" and "as bent as they come". With his drawn handsome face and his tall, straight bearing, he looked eccentric and caught all eyes as he carried his long walking stick like an officer's baton, firmly under his arm, and he held the eye of his clients with an unblinking gaze. He was not a man to cross.

The little room, in which Parkinson and Leander were now seated, was surrounded on all sides, from floor to ceiling, with books of every description, all carefully indexed and with neat, black and white labels indicating the subject matter of the books by shelves. They made the room feel heavy and the dark cases contrasted with the centre light which now illuminated the Leander letter's copied sheets, which Leander had stolen from Harry Guest's bedroom. The pages lay beside an open notebook.

Referring to the letter Parkinson said, "Christopher Marlowe is my favourite, laddy. After he was awarded his B.A. degree at Cambridge, and in the ten remaining years of his life, he wrote the two parts – immensely long both of them – of *Tamburlaine the Great, Dr. Faustus, The Jew of Malta, Edward the Second, The Massacre of Paris, Dido, Queen of Carthage* and much else besides, including poetry and translations. It was a remarkable feat to produce such magnificent poetry on such a scale in such a comparatively short space of time."

Leander said, "I remember him in Higher Cert. at school. He invented blank verse, didn't he?"

"It's interesting that you should make that point. You know, dear boy, there's a memorial to Marlowe in St. Nicholas Church at Deptford. In Marlowe's day Deptford was a village outside London. The memorial was erected by some unknown person as recently as 1919. There's an engraving on a brass plate." He peered down at his notebook and read aloud from it: "To the Immortal Memorial of Christopher Marlowe M.A. The Founder of Grandiloquent Blank Verse."

Leander nodded and Parkinson went on to say, "Shakespeare was truly influenced by him. It was Michael Drayton, that staggeringly prolific, Elizabethan poet, who wrote a thumb-nail sketch of Marlowe in verse, a little cameo of the man, if I can remember it, that is."

Then he recited it from memory:

"Next Marlowe, bathed in the Thespian springs,

Had in him those brave translunary things
That your first poets had; his raptures were
All air and fire, which made his verses clear,
For that fine madness still he did retain,
Which rightly should possess a poet's brain."

As he finished, he rose from his seat, adding "The Bard carried forward what Marlowe conceived, laddy."

He took a book from one of the shelves. "This find of yours is enthralling," he said. Returning to the table, he sat and opened the book, flicking through the dusty volume, sneezing at the waft of dust from the pages and halting to quote from it.

"Here is the arch-betrayer," he said. "The man, who could have originated the saying that 'he would sell his grandmother's soul for sixpence' I mean, Richard Baines, who constantly stirred up trouble for Kit Marlowe. He was a public informer, a menace."

Parkinson checked the book and said, "Listen to this. Baines is accusing Marlowe and referring to a particular witness as follows, *That on(e) Ric Cholmey hath Confessed that he was persuaded by Marlowe's Reasons to become an Atheist.*"

Leander said airily, "Yet these are only baubles of information about a genius, whom some scholars believe would have become a greater poet than Shakespeare, if he had survived."

"But he wouldn't have survived, laddy. They had him sewn up." Parkinson riffled through the pages of the book. "What about this? Baines once more, of course, on Marlowe, alleging words which the poet had been heard to say, *That the first beginning of religoun was only to keep men in awe.* In Elizabeth's day you couldn't come out with that sort of stuff too often and get away with it. And they were hard on his tail. Quite unlike Shakespeare who always kept his nose clean."

Part 3: Return to Cornwall: September 1946

Parkinson stood up again and said, "Right at the end of Marlowe's life, Richard Baines prepared his string of accusations against the poet, which he passed to the Privy Council. The informer at work. And he also made a copy of the list which was intended for Queen Elizabeth to see. Vicious so-and-so. It is headed:

Copye of Marloes
blasphemyes
As sent to her Highness."

Then he replaced the book and peered down a row of volumes until he found what he was seeking and returned to the table with another work.

"This will interest you," he announced. "The original notice of Marlowe's inquest." He turned the pages and held a finger directly between the two of them.

"This is it: *Kent Inquisition Indented taken at Deptford Strand in the aforesaid County of Kent within the verge on the first day of June in the thirty fifth year of the reign of Elizabeth by the grace of God of England, France and Ireland Queen defender of the faith* and so it goes on."

Parkinson smiled and asked, "Do you know what the verge was?"

Leander shook his head.

Parkinson said, "Really it meant a distance of twelve miles round Elizabeth and her court. And so Deptford was within the verge. Well now, the coroner's name was William Danby and... ah, you look. Read for yourself what the coroner's notice had to say about the dreadful episode."

He passed the book over to Leander, holding the pages apart with one hand and pointing with the forefinger of the other. Leander pulled the book towards him over the soft cloth and read the report of the jurymen to the coroner, dated Friday, June 1st, 1593, *how Ingram ffrysar, Nicholas*

Was There Ever Seen Such Villainy?

Skeres and Robert Poley met Christopher Morley at Deptford Strand in a room in Eleanor Bull's tavern.

The jurymen learned how the four men *passed the time together and dined and after dinner were in quiet sort together there and walked in the garden belonging to the said house until the sixth hour after noon of the same day and then returned from the said garden to the room aforesaid and there together and in company supped: and after supper the said Ingram and Christopher Morley were in speech and uttered one to the other divers malicious words for the reason that they could not be at one nor agree about the payment of the sum of pence, that is le recknynge, there; and the said Christopher Morley then lying upon a bed in the room where they supped, and moved with anger against...*

Leander looked up. "What is known about Marlowe's character?" he asked. "Was he quick-tempered?"

"Oh yes, yes – I don't believe that's in doubt, my boy, but I always think the words lurking behind the words of that document – if you see what I mean – ring out a truth of their own. But, go on – go on..."

The young man continued reading from where Marlowe was moved with anger *against the said Ingram ffrysar upon the words as aforesaid between them. And the said Ingram then and there sitting in the room aforesaid with his back towards the bed where the said Christopher Morley was then lying, sitting near the bed, that is, nere the bed, and with the front part of his body towards the table and the aforesaid Nicholas Skeres and Robert Poley sitting on either side of the said Ingram in such a manner that the same Ingram ffrysar in no wise could take flight; it so befell that the said Christopher Morley on a sudden and of his malice towards the said Ingram aforethought, then and there maliciously drew the dagger of the said Ingram which was at his back, and with the same dagger the said*

Part 3: Return to Cornwall: September 1946

Christopher Morley then and there maliciously gave the aforesaid Ingram two wounds on his head...

Raising his head Leander said, "I thought you told me once that Elizabethan men, when attacking during a knife fight, would grasp their daggers by the blade end and, in this reversed position would batter their opponents with the blunt end of the knife."

"Well done, laddy, but the witness statements to the Coroner were obviously invented to protect Ingram from justice. There was a good reason for brawlers, then, to use what to us seems to be a dangerous variation on knife fighting."

"How do you mean?"

"I mean that the penalties for injuring a man in such a fight could be lengthy imprisonment and all sorts of other possibilities: whipping, torture and dreadfully inhumane prison conditions where death from disease was on the cards."

"Yes, I see. So they fought with knives reversed, and striking with the dagger's pommel. In that way they would hope to limit any harm caused to the opponent. Whereas – obviously – presenting the blade direct would be highly dangerous."

Leander glanced at the page again.

"There's another thing I don't understand. It says here that Kit *drew the dagger of the said Ingram which was at his back*. I suppose he took it from the scabbard in Ingram's belt from behind him. But, surely he would instinctively have used his own dagger? Why lean over and alert Ingram to his intended assault by taking his dagger? Look at it this way, if he really decided – even in temper – to seize Ingram's dagger from the back, he must have been concerned that he might fumble in this attempt to grasp the pommel. There's no logic in this story."

Brucey made no comment, and Leander cast his eyes over the rest of the report from the point where *Christopher*

117

Morley had inflicted two head wounds on Ingram's head... *of the length of two inches and of the depth of a quarter of an inch: whereupon the said Ingram, in fear of being slain, and sitting in the manner aforesaid between the said Nicholas Skeres and Robert Poley so that he could not in any wise get away, in his own defence and for the saving of his life, then and there struggled with the said Christopher Morley to get back from him his dagger aforesaid; and so it befell in that affray that the said Ingram, in defence of his life, with the dagger aforesaid of the value of 12d. gave the said Christopher then and there a mortal wound over his right eye of the depth of two inches and of the width of one inch: of which mortal wound the aforesaid Christopher Morley then and there instantly died.*

Leander quickly asked, "What about the dagger *of the value of 12d.?* Where did it come from? It was used by Ingram who, we know from the story, had already lost his own dagger to Kit. If Ingram struggled with Marlowe *to get back from him his dagger,* there is nothing said about his regaining it. On the contrary the report concludes that *Ingram could not get away from him.* So what can we make of this dagger of *value of 12d.?* In my view it's all cock and bull Elizabethan eye-wash!"

Brucey replied, "It's certainly a mystery. And, I've something to add, dear boy, tell me what on earth was he doing lying on a bed behind his assembled buddies at the table? There's no suggestion that he was drunk. And, if he had attacked, knowing the ferocity of the law on the subject, he would automatically have struck out with his dagger's pommel – if he did indeed attack at all. It is the pommel which would have knocked out Ingram without any need to cut the man's head open as described. Do you see, laddy?"

"You're right, Brucey, the story is overflowing with apparent contradictions and queries."

Brucey was more direct.

"It's all rather different, isn't it? Not in accord with the first Leander Penhalion's record of events; as far as his 1593 letter goes. Leander states that those devils, Poley, ffrysar – it later became spelt by the way, as Frizer – and Skeres tried to torture a confession from Marlowe and that Marlowe – you see that his name is wrongly printed as Morley – was killed, when he tried to defend himself from them. Quite the opposite to what they alleged. There's a wicked twist for you: the way of the world, of course."

"It's dreadful!" Leander said with feeling as he pushed the book across the table.

The two men were both silent, the only sound to be heard being from the flick of the book's crisp pages which Parkinson turned.

Presently Leander spoke again. He said, "In spite of this surprising detail, there's generally really too little known about the short life of Marlowe and even less about Shakespeare. Why was that?"

"It was the plague, you see. It was rampant in London especially. That's why there's a paucity of information about Kit Marlowe himself. But – we have his verse."

He stayed silent for a moment and then began to recite, in a gravely tone:

"Stand still, you ever-moving spheres of Heaven,
That time may cease, and midnight never come!"

As he finished, he said, "Marlowe's Faustus about to depart to eternal damnation and attempting to put off the fatal hour."

Unhurriedly he closed the book and placed it back on the shelf.

"Well, I'll tell you what we'll do. We must carry on as before. Keep an eye on them. They must lead us to the crock of gold. Save us the trouble. After all, even if we knew the whereabouts of the cave, we wouldn't know the whereabouts of the gold, laddy, would we? And look how well you've done already – quite astonishing – to bring this letter!"

"You mean I must go on keeping a look out. But don't forget I'm working at the farm still. It was difficult enough to get here today. I'm away from things at home most of each day. And I get back late. We've been over all this before."

"But you live on the spot. That's how the letter was heard of. That's how you were successful. And you must go on as you have done so far, keeping your eyes and ears open. Contact me again at once on the 'phone if you come across the smallest clue. Laddy, there is no other way. And if we get a gleam of hope, I'll be down with you right away. Perhaps not the Kemp-Reydon Guest House again, but you can advise me where to stay when the time comes."

Perhaps not the Kemp-Reydon Guest House, Leander repeated to himself. I should think Mrs. Robinson would never have him back after all the fuss Brucey made, when he returned drunk after the dance that night.

Leander had witnessed the angry exchange between Brucey and Mrs. Robinson, when he had called to pick up his friend the next day; it had all been about some damage which Brucey had caused in the night. Afterwards Brucey had been in a sullen mood, angry over the previous evening's debacle. Leander had offered to take him to St. Aubyn's station to catch the London train, using his old Austin, a recent gift from Jean.

Brucey had demanded that they should call at Red Bluff, in spite of the mist which they encountered on the way, because he had some ridiculous idea of arranging a "communication system" whereby, on the twenty third of September – when they believed that Guest would attempt to reach the cave – one of them would signal from the top of Red Bluff point to the other, who would be waiting on Western Cove beach. As soon as the observer above saw

Guest entering the cave, he would signal to the one below to speed after Guest with the outboard motor attached to the second dinghy.

Leander said, "But, Brucey we must stick together. It's the only way. You see. Brucey, I believe it's important that we stay together. Guest is no easy target."

Brucey began to show his usual signs of rising anger, when Leander acted decisively, settling the matter by adding, "There's another point. We'll need two of us to launch the boat, when the time comes to return, especially if there's any delay and we meet the turning tide."

Brucey had calmed down, realising the sense of Leander's words. He said, "In that case our signal will be the sight of Guest's shape as he rows out of sight round Red Bluff. We follow then."

So, the absurd reconnaissance on Red Bluff in the mist had at least given Leander the unexpected bonus of the agreement that they would act together when the time came to follow Guest to the cave.

IX

Harry spent most of the day walking. He took sandwiches with him and, as the tide was going out, he kept to the seashore, from time to time scrambling over rocks lying in his path, and later, across the obstacle presented by St. Hilda's Rise, a snaking finger of land which protruded into the sea about a mile down the coast. In due course he reached St. Minnion's point, some six miles to the West. He ate his lunch, broodily chewing mouthfuls of cheese and pickle as he occasionally cast stones from the cliff back into the sea. Once he eagerly brought his binoculars to his eyes on hearing a shrill bird call and seeing three oystercatchers flying low over the sea, black and white, dark plumage on top and white underneath, with orange bills. The birds swooped down to the beach and, immediately on landing, began to search for shell-fish with their long bills as they perched on stately legs. He soon found his mind clouding over again; he desperately wanted to be with Manon and the memory of the dark-haired girl constantly returned however hard he tried to turn his thoughts elsewhere.

At length he set off to return by the cliff path which took him past meadows filled with wild flowers. The sight of them reminded him that Alex would, most likely, be able to give him the names of all the different plants growing there, if he could tell her exactly what he had seen. As the miles went by, he therefore tried, as he passed them, to memorise their appearance so as to be able to ask her to name them. In fact the flowers, as he noticed, were sometimes in widely scattered splashes of colour, sometimes in dense clusters and sometimes in splendid isolation, everywhere exuding their mottled scents on the balmy breeze. They included autumn squill with its wide-spread, green leaves, the gorgeous, yellow horned poppy, yellow tree lupin, originally a native of the Californian coast, the vivid purple of tree mallow from the Mediterranean, more yellow petals in the shape of golden samphire, narrow leaved bird's foot trefoil, Cornish heath, the dazzling rose-pink of rosebay willowherb, or fire weed, which was at the time popular with people in the blitzed cities, where it flourished on the bombed sites; and, on the side of the path next to the sea, in abundance by the rocks, pretty, pink thrift, sometimes called sea pink. When he met Alex again, she told him the names of each of the flowers, which he had seen, as he described them to her. With the passage of time, as he walked on, he did not at once realise what a beguiling effect the countryside was having on him, but when he returned, he arrived at the Red House with raised spirits. As he leaped up the stairs, two at a time, however, he recalled Manon's image and he hoped eagerly that he would see her, when he went with Vivian to The Ship that evening, but first of all he would have a refreshing bath and change of clothes.

Manon was not at The Ship. After dinner Harry listened in the lounge to Joe Loss and his band on the radio, followed by the weather forecast which preceded the nine o'clock news. The announcer predicted continuing sunshine until the weekend, when gales were expected all along the south-western coast. Harry noted that it would be windy on the 23rd September.

It was not long after that he went upstairs to bed, calling out, 'Goodnight', as he left the room. In bed he read several chapters of Alan Moorhead's *Trilogy*, the section dealing with the journalist's experiences during the war in Italy, at the same times and places that Harry had also served, so that he was able to disagree with some of the writer's conclusions. At last he leaned over to the bedside lamp and switched it off. In less than two minutes he was sleeping peacefully.

He lay quite still. Something had wakened him. He heard the sound again, muffled as if far off, or as if somehow cushioned. It was, faintly as he heard it, a woman's laugh. Harry stepped quickly out of bed and crossed to the open window, where he leaned out as far as he could and listened. There was no sound from outside. He heard it again, this time from the direction of the wall against which his bed stood. As he looked he was surprised to see a light, which he had not noticed previously, gleaming high up by the ceiling.

He stared at the light, as he listened to see if the laugh would be repeated. Then he climbed on the bed and placing both hands against the wall, stood with shoulders bent and head against the ceiling above the light. He saw at once that rotten wood and crumbling plaster had given way, perhaps as a result of gradual deterioration over the centuries. Whatever the cause, he found an opening as large as a half brick, impossible to detect from below because of the mouldings. From the opening he could see into the neighbouring bedroom, on to a limited sector of the room, in the centre of which a bed was placed against the opposite wall. There must have been a similar light next door to the one in his room, because it was bathed in the same orange glow.

As he continued to peer into the room, his thoughts wandered back to a day in Italy during the war, when he

124

was attached to a special patrol unit which had penetrated behind the enemy lines. On that occasion he had observed Germans, who had occupied a pastoral valley. They had moved about their duties, receiving ammunition supplies, cleaning weapons, cooking and generally behaving as if they were on manoeuvres back in Germany. It had been a strange feeling which he had experienced then – almost of power, as if the Germans had been in his power as he had watched the unconcerned behaviour of the troops, yet knowing that they had been completely unaware of being spied on. He felt exactly the same sensation now, the sensation known to the voyeur, but spiced with an accelerating excitement.

It was difficult in his cramped position to keep the small image in focus, or indeed to make out exactly what was in his vision on the bed. Each time he moved, which he did frequently on the soft-sprung mattress, he saw a different piece of the room, but always restricted by the ragged channel which penetrated from one wall to the other. Suddenly there was a rapid movement and a tall, sun-tanned, nude, male figure filled his field of view for several seconds before shifting sideways. As the man appeared, Harry saw Leander's smiling face. He was puzzled; this was not Leander's bedroom; his room was in the family block on the other side of the house. But, of course, he remembered that he had changed bedrooms for Jean. For a moment he flexed his hands which had become stiff. A quick glance at his watch showed 2.30 a.m. When he looked back, he heard the girl's laugh once more. As he took in the scene this time, he saw the girl's body. She also was naked, lying face down on the bed; he could see dark hair resting on slim shoulders, the deep curve of her back and the prominent hips. As he watched, she stretched and glanced over her shoulders at her own sensuous body in unconscious imitation of the Venus Callipyge. The sound of her voice had been familiar; and before she turned her face again towards Leander, who was out of sight, Harry

125

knew that it was Manon. Her cheeks were flushed with excitement and she was smiling, too.

Harry slowly let himself crumple back onto his bed, where he lay still, gradually letting his angry jealousy subside. It was not long after that the muted sounds next door ceased and the faint light was extinguished. It was however a long time before Harry fell asleep, but he did eventually sleep as the fingers of dawn light crept across the sky.

Harry wakened with a headache. After he had washed his face vigorously in cold water, shaved and dressed, he felt better, more angry now than jealous following the surprising scene he had witnessed in the night, but already curiosity had taken over. Before going downstairs for breakfast, he stopped outside the door to the neighbouring bedroom which was ajar. Nobody was in the corridor or on the landing at the end of it, so he pushed the door open and put his head round it. The room was empty and the bedclothes had been left neatly in place as if no one had slept there. He stepped inside and cast his eyes up at the damaged moulding above. He could see the vent, but it merged with the cracked plaster without drawing attention to the opening.

He thought about Leander. He must have brought Manon to the room very late, without his parents' knowledge and let her out before dawn. But how had she returned to the farm? Perhaps Leander had driven her back, or she had borrowed her brother's car and then parked it further along the road from the Red House, so as not to alert the household in the early hours, when she started up. Leander would then have returned to his own room and slept off the remaining hours.

It was Alex's day off. She had planned to go into Plymouth with her father to shop, but that was to be later in the morning: first she had agreed to go for a walk with Harry. After breakfast they set off together down the familiar path to Red Bluff. As they strolled on to the rising ground, they were accompanied by a curious, little bird which flew with a swooping flight from bush to bush. It was almost as if they had a pet, so closely did the bird keep up with them. As they paused on the track, the bird halted too, sitting on a nearby shrub so that they could see its striped, olive and dark brown markings and its streaked, white breast.

"It's a meadow pipit," said Alex as the bird flew off on a sideways course until it disappeared.

They walked to the top of the Bluff and came to a stop halfway between the commencement of the flat ground and the cut-off drop in the centre of the pincer of land at the apex. The sun was warm and the breeze from the sea was cool. They sat together looking at the views of the sea on either side of the Bluff.

Harry said, "I never told you how I got on, when I went to Plymouth yesterday. I only told you about the earlier episode on Red Bluff."

"Did you get to the library?" asked Alex.

"Yes, and there was plenty about Christopher Marlowe. He would apparently have been a rival to Shakespeare if he had lived. What a tragedy! And isn't it sad that it should all have come about over some absurd argument in a tavern as to who should pay the bill for dinner – as history relates, that is, but not according to the first Leander's letter."

There was a silence which Alex broke, asking, "Did you find anything else?"

"Actually I copied out one extraordinary piece involving Kit Marlowe as I thought you'd like to read it. I'll show you some time."

"I'd love to see it."

"But there were other things too. Especially on Cellini."

Harry described the colour illustration which he had seen of Cellini's salt cellar, made for the King of France. "It looks absolutely smashing – gorgeous, gold figures reclining away from each other. If Marlowe's goldsmith was Cellini – and I don't see why the treasure should not be by him – what a masterpiece it will be. Isn't that great?"

Alex replied, "Yes. And I've heard about the salt cellar too. As you've seen in the picture of it, the male and female figures have their legs entwined together."

"I wondered about that."

"It's supposed to represent the combination of the elements, and it's called 'Neptune and Ceres'."

Despite all these interesting points Alex added that she was not excited about it.

"I'm quite sure it's no longer there, wherever it is. But, I do worry about the dangers involved in going to the cave. What about the weather?"

"The forecast says it'll be windy." He brushed aside this issue by adding, "You'd expect that around this particular date. We'll hear what's reported nearer the day. Meanwhile I've still got to get hold of a powerful torch to light up the cavities inside the cave. And, as I've said before, I also need a crowbar for prising out the casket – in case it has become stuck between rocks over the years. You see," he said with a grin, "I've got to be optimistic."

"I could get them in Plymouth," offered Alex, but she quickly corrected herself. "Oh no, of course I can't. Daddy will be with me."

"It's kind of you – no. I'll get them. I might even be lucky at the St. Aubyn stores. All sorts of pre-war things turn up unexpectedly in shops in spite of the shortages everywhere."

Alex, who was lying back on the grass, said, "The sun's hot down here." She twisted her wrist to see her watch. "Help! I'd no idea we'd been so long. I must dash. I don't want to keep Daddy waiting."

They stood up and, as they parted, kissed briefly, as friends do. Harry watched her receding form and her red hair streaming in the wind.

Part 3: Return to Cornwall: September 1946

When he started to walk South on the flat spine of the Bluff, his thoughts switched to Manon. In his mind he saw the seductive girl in the orange light, smiling, flushed as she waited for Leander in the bedroom so close to him. Leander of all people! From Leander his thoughts went to Parkinson. There was the unanswered question of the relationship between the three of them: Parkinson, Leander and Manon. Could they be working together? Impossible! He recalled the outraged expression on Manon's face as she flung the contents of her glass in Parkinson's face at the dance. In no circumstances could she be working with them as a team. But still, it could have been Manon who had been in the public bar at The Ship, when Alex and he discussed the discovery of the letter; and, on last night's evidence, she could have passed the information on to Leander. Indeed, if it was Manon who overheard them, what was she most likely to do if she was Leander's lover?

Parkinson and Leander's friendship was well established. If Manon had told Leander the story of the treasure trove, who would be the first person whom he would consult? Obviously, Parkinson who had at hand all the expertise of the family's art-antique enterprise in Soho. And it was surely no coincidence that Parkinson had appeared in Lavington on the night of the dance. Harry's thoughts drifted back to Manon, as he recalled their passionate encounter in the back room at the town hall, and then he remembered what he had seen from his bedroom last night. "She must be a nymphomaniac!" he said aloud, kicking at tufts of grass as he walked.

He was heading for the end of Red Bluff, where he wanted to examine the appearance of underwater rocks from above. If he could estimate roughly where he believed the entrance to the cave was situated, it would be helpful to know if there were any rocky hazards in the area from the point of view of landing and launching. The sea was calm but the breeze kept the gulls and the fulmars drifting, the latter stiff winged as they made their wheeling turns over the water. Some cormorants were active too, plunging into the sea seeking out flat fish, while other cormorants rested on the giant rocks about the foot of the Bluff's extremity. When Harry came to the pincer head, he stood cautiously, staring at the far off rocks. With his binoculars he searched both arms of the pincers and the rocky centrepiece, where he thought the cave lay. His eye moved over the clear blue-mauve coloured water and onto the point, where the massive crags rose from the breaking sea. There he saw what looked like a shelf of rock protruding under water for several yards out to sea.

When he had finished his brief reconnaissance, he stepped back to look at the sparkling view before sauntering down the Bluff on the descending path. As he went he noticed a white patch in the grass on the right hand side, away from the sea. When he came closer, the white patch became the clothing of a sun-tanned girl. As Harry approached, a solitary, waiting figure rose to greet him. It was Manon, dressed all in white, wearing a blouse, shorts and, in contrast, a scarlet belt which accentuated her small waist and emphasised her wide hips. Her dark hair and brown skin appeared to be even darker against her white clothes. She was a picture of health.

As Harry regarded her, he was amazed at the chameleon-like change which she could effect from erotic temptress of the previous night to the girl, who stood before him. She was quite different. Although she was strikingly attractive, yet there was about her a demure quality, and the ready smile was absent from her mouth, almost as if she had somehow been hurt. Harry felt his anger evaporating as he looked into her eyes.

"Hello, Harry. I hoped I'd find you up here."

"Why?" he asked abruptly.

She said, "I saw you with Alex", as if that explained her presence.

Harry stiffened. "Do you mind if I meet her?"

He was surprised to see that she seemed to be disconcerted by his question.

"No, Harry, no. I didn't mean that."

They looked at each other for a moment too long.

Manon sensed Harry's prickly mood, although she could not possibly know the reason for it. She continued her demure role, the reverse of the quixotic and bold Manon whom he also knew. Yet, when she came up to him on the path, she deftly flung her arms around him, as if compelled by an insatiable urge. Pulling his head down to her mouth, she pressed herself to him and kissed him passionately. Taken off guard, Harry at first responded to her kiss, but he gradually unlocked her fingers and brought her hands firmly but gently between them. He stared at her without saying a word.

Seeming to ignore his action, Manon said, "There's another dance at Lavington tomorrow. It's a mid-week special in aid of the Red Cross. Will you come with me?"

He could not understand her, and in a moment all his anger returned.

"No. Thank you, Manon," he said with exaggerated courtesy. Without even turning back, he walked briskly away from her and down the hill.

X

Day after day there was brilliant sunshine, and this day was as hot as ever. During the afternoon Harry returned to the Red House from the beach because he had a number of letters to write.

Upstairs he filled the bathtub and lay in the water letting his thoughts stray. Another sunny day. Brilliant. Must have been like this before the war. My parents always talking abut the summers when they were young, in the 1920s. Just right. Now, I'll drive along the coast road West of Lavington, and lie on the shore. I'll take the original Leander letter. What a bore to have to copy out another one – after the burglary. Well, I'll have a long, hard look at it. Every detail, again. Make sure I've got the picture absolutely correctly.

He returned to his bedroom and put on a clean shirt, shorts, knee-length socks and plimsolls. As he left the house, he jumped quickly into his old Minx, letting out a gasp as the back of his thighs touched the scorching leather of the car seats. Instantly he opened all the windows and also wound out the windscreen itself before starting the engine. Then he opened the cubby hole, slipped the Leander letter in and closed the door.

132

Part 3: Return to Cornwall: September 1946

The road from Red House to Lavington went due North over the ridge and into the long, sweeping valley on the far side, leading to the high point overlooking the rolling, green countryside which dipped to the sea in the South. Shortly the road joined the main thoroughfare to which, further back to the East, the track from Moorland Farm was connected; but Harry turned left on to the westward stretch to Lavington. After a mile the road swung steeply round to run back for about three-quarters of a mile; just before recoiling on itself, it sloped into a hairpin bend and then ran almost straight toward the town. He drove round the first, long corner and then, relieved to have completed the hairpin bend at a snail's pace, he accelerated up through the synchromesh gears to 50 m.p.h. Suddenly, he saw the figure of a girl standing in the middle of the road directly ahead of the car; one moment the road was clear and then the girl was before him, holding up both hands in an imperative signal for him to stop.

"Oh, my God!" he cried out, thinking that it would be impossible to avoid running her down.

Immediately he slammed on the car brakes with all his strength. The car responded with a scream of tyres on tarmac and a strong smell of burning rubber, as it veered sharply to the nearside of the road, out of control. The girl reacted fast too, moving to her right to side-step the oncoming car, but still the car was heading for her. Harry corrected the steering again, heaving the wheel hard over to the right, trying to bring the car into the centre of the road, but it lurched across to the opposite bank, where it came to a standstill and the engine cut out.

His heart was thumping. He automatically turned off the ignition key and leaped out. The girl was lying in a heap on the far side of the road, but she did not seem to be hurt and she was beginning to stand up.

"You stupid woman!" Harry shouted. "You almost killed us both."

Dry-mouthed, he watched the girl as she threw her hair back from her face.

Very coolly Manon said, "I'm sorry, Harry. I misjudged your speed."

Already he was calmer. "Why did you do it?" he asked in an exasperated tone of voice.

"I've got a puncture," she said lamely.

"A puncture!" he repeated.

"Yes, over there." Manon pointed to her bicycle which lay out of sight in the long grass several yards behind the spot where the car was resting at an acute angle to the bank.

He nodded. "Tell me about it in a minute. How are you? Are you alright?"

She smiled. "Yes, thanks to your driving."

"Don't give me that. What happened?"

"I saw you – or rather I recognised your car in the distance. You remember the Saturday Dance at Lavington Town Hall?"

"I shall never forget it."

"There you are. I saw you drive up with the Penhalion family and Vivian's car too. You parked outside the Hall and Vivian parked beside you. So I know your car."

"And? What next?"

"I saw you from the top of the hill there." She indicated the low ridge rising above the shrubs on the other side of the car, where he could see that a footpath led to the summit.

"It was luck, really. I turned when I got to the top and glanced back – as you came into sight. I quickly judged that you would have to slow down for the long corner and the hairpin bend, and I estimated that I had time to run down the road here and thumb a lift into Lavington," she said. "Am I forgiven?"

Harry thought: Has she forgiven me for snubbing her on Red Bluff? But he said, "There's nothing to forgive. I'm sorry I spoke to you like that just now."

He opened up the small car boot and folded Manon's bicycle, but when he lifted it into the boot, only part of the machine would fit inside. He therefore secured it with rope which he kept in the back of the car, leaving the lid of the boot partly open.

"Come on," he said. "Do you know where you can get the puncture repaired?"

"Jackson's. It's the first garage you come to, on the outskirts of town."

The car started and when they reached the garage, Manon found that the puncture could be repaired and ready for collection later in the afternoon. Harry then asked if she would like to have tea with him at the "Cosy Café" in the square.

"I'd love it, Harry."

He drove to the square and parked outside the café.

"Do you mind, Manon?" he asked as he stepped out, holding up the envelopes in his hand. "I won't be long, I've got to get stamps and post these."

She smiled and shook her head, and Harry went over to the Post Office.

When he returned, Manon was still sitting in the passenger seat of the car, so he walked round to the pavement and opened the door for her. The inside of the tea shop was shabby, but the owner, who had been a land army girl, was fat, rosy-cheeked and friendly. She gave them a warm welcome and soon brought tea and scones with jam and cream. Drinking from the pink floral cups, they both relaxed.

"Really, Harry, it was silly of me. I didn't want to miss you and I got all muddled with my bike as I emerged from the path on to the road."

"Never mind. But it must be about twelve miles from the farm to the town. Were you going to do the twenty four mile round trip on your bike?"

She laughed. "No, Maurice gave me a lift in the farm car up to the Red House junction. He turned back as he was late for an appointment with a farmer friend in the other direction. I'm getting a lift back this evening."

"And why push your bike over the hills?"

"It's like a police enquiry," she said with a smile. "I decided to take the path over the hills, because it's a short cut and easier than lugging the bike with its puncture all the way round by road. It happened shortly after Maurice left me. I was livid."

So, it was all explained. The two chatted, exchanging news. Harry listened attentively to her voice as she spoke.

"Are you going to be free this evening?" he asked.

"No. I'm meeting a friend. But what about tomorrow?"

"Yes, I'd like that. Where would be best for you?"

"What about Western Cove, on the beach by Red Bluff?"

"That'll do for me. What do you say ten-ish?"

She nodded her head, and they stood up to go.

"Thank you, Harry, for the tea – and the lift."

She pursed her lips in a smile.

"It was nice seeing you, Manon. On Friday, then. Red Bluff at ten or so."

Harry paid the bill as she waved and left the tea shop.

Just after her departure, he froze where he was standing. He had remembered the last pages of the Leander letter. In view of all that had passed, how could he have been so careless, when he went to the post? Fancy leaving the pages in the unlocked cubby hole with Manon on her own. He rushed outside. Dragging open the car door, he slipped into the passenger seat and pulled open the cubby hole door. The Leander papers were lying there.

Harry drove West on the coast road with which he was unfamiliar. Less spectacular than the seaside region of Red Bluff, it had its own softer appeal with gorse land fringing the pallid, sandy beaches. He found a place to park on the turf, where the sea lapped one hundred yards off. Making himself comfortable in a sand dune with thick marram grass to support his back he settled down to deal with the chore of re-writing his modernised version of Leander's letter to his father at the Red Inn. When he had finished and checked it, he let his mind wander on the cave project.

Let's see exactly what the problems are likely to be. First, landing the dinghy. Will have to judge the right moment for the dinghy's approach from the sea. A hard pull on the oars and then ready as the boat sweeps in. Hope it lands safely. Don't want to overturn in the water. A lot will depend on the weather. When I've landed I must pull the dinghy well clear of the waves – and leave it for a sharp launch. No hanging about. Then enter the cave and start the search. Essential I don't get the timing wrong. The incoming tide could easily capsize the boat as the driving waves crash against the rocky entrance. Boat could be shattered in no time. So – I must concentrate all my thoughts on getting the job done as soon as possible. Afterwards return at speed. No mistakes. Inside I'm lucky. Leander's letter could hardly be more precise about where to go: the rock crack which Leander describes. And that, I hope, is that.

Returning to the car he was confident about his plans to visit the cave on the 23rd September. He drove to The Ship where he called in for a drink. Just as he was leaving, he noticed the back view of a young couple as they turned up the lane beside the Town Hall. It was Leander and Manon. Of course, Manon had said she was getting a lift back. They were wheeling what looked like Manon's bicycle between them.

That night Harry retired early, a little depressed, partly at seeing Manon with Leander. What can she see in him? And what if she had managed to read the last pages of Leander's letter? Silly to worry – the pages were untouched. Or were they? What a relief it was to find the complete letter there, the vital original, after he had parted from Manon – but she could have glanced at the last pages. Where exactly did I leave the letter? On the side nearest the steering wheel. But, where was it when I returned on my own? When I flung open the cubby door, the letter was on the opposite side, beside the passenger door, or so I thought. If Manon read the important details at the end of the letter showing where the casket lies, she would have told Leander, who would have passed it on to Brucey.

In the end he persuaded himself it didn't matter. There was nothing he could do about it. Despite his ambivalent feelings towards her, he fell asleep looking forward to seeing Manon for the first time by appointment.

XI

Answering the telephone's bell in London, Brucey picked up the black receiver and said, "Parkinson speaking."

He heard the clatter of coins from a call box, as Leander said, "Brucey. It's me. And I've got news for you."

"Leander. Great of you to call. What's it about?"

"I'm in Cornwall of course. And here I bumped into Manon of all people."

Her paused to see if there was any comment. But Brucey was barely able to conceal his jealousy of the fact that Leander had spoken to Manon.

Guessing the cause of the silence at the other end of the 'phone, Leander put on his bland style, saying, "She was walking through Lavington where we met, and she told me she had been with Guest."

"What! What's she found out? Tell me."

"Well, here it is. What do you know? She said she had what she called a "fleeting" glance and read part of the ancestor Leander's last pages – the ones which were missing from the main letter which I picked up in Guest's bedroom."

"Tell me!" Brucey's voice was strained. "Don't mess about, boy. Tell me what did it say? Is there any more information for us?"

"Just a minute, Brucey," Leander replied gently. "I'll tell you. Manon didn't have much time and the pages were not all that easy to read. Anyway she took a quick look at them while Guest left her alone in his car. She found them in the cubby hole, you see. No wonder Guest made a copy of the original letter. It was very hard to read. What with that, and also having to keep an eye out for Guest's return to the car, she could only make out two, brief bits of additional news."

"What news for God's sake?" Brucey was clenching and un-clenching his hands as Leander imagined.

"It's a Cellini in the cave."

There was a short silence and Brucey's hands were stilled.

"Cellini," he echoed. "Cellini. You know there's only one example of his work in gold left to the world – and that's the famous salt cellar of the King of France. There may be one or two others, but they cannot be fully authenticated. Very sad. But there was always the chronic problem of thieving philistines eager to melt down great artistic monuments to gain the gold itself for their greedy pockets. Especially sad in Cellini's case – he was the greatest goldsmith of all time. Just think of our loss. But now think of what could be our gain!"

Leander had been trying to intervene. Now he said, "There's more to come. Manon told me that there were instructions about where the masterpiece lies – although all she could read was this: the box is in a crevice in the centre of a raised, rocky platform at the rear of the cave."

The telephone call was interrupted by "pips", and there was a pause while Leander fed more coins into the 'phone-box.

140

Part 3: Return to Cornwall: September 1946

Brucey then continued, "That is really good news – makes the prospects more promising." The tone of his voice changed as he added, "But I warn you. We'll need to have all the luck in the game. If the treasure's still there – and that's another issue – it will be guarded by the sea, and my guess is that it will be really hard to find too. It's not going to be easy – any of it, laddy."

Leander felt himself bristling at the dolorous response to the amazing new data. He said, "But what a great surprise it is! We know what we're looking for and now we know just what to expect inside the cave. We can have a go – on our own – can't we? We even have a good idea where to look."

Brucey's voice became more sombre. "Listen, laddy. Be careful! It's better to let Guest lead us. Think about it. He can test the conditions at the cave entrance for us. If it's too rough, let him get into trouble. And he will have time to sort himself out. We'll let him do our dirty work for us, dear boy." He paused and then went on with emphasis, "This is what we are going to do. We keep a vigil on the twenty third. And when Guest goes there, we use the outboard motor, as we agreed, and we follow him in the second dinghy as soon as he turns the corner of the Bluff."

"But no delays," said Leander. "It's vital we follow up rapidly. And, also, we must keep in mind the danger of the tide."

Brucey did not reply at once. When he did, his voice was warm. "A very good warning. And if for whatever reason he fails this year – or if we fail this year – there's always the possibility of another go in the Spring next year – the vernal tide – sometime in April."

"If that happened, we'd have more time to get ready, especially now we've got more facts to go on. We might even get outside help."

"No!" Brucey's roar came down the line. "No. At least, only as a last resort. But, in any case, let's concentrate on this year. We've done the planning outline. Just enough

141

stores for our frugal needs – as we planned, against any possible emergency. So, we keep an observation post in the shelter and watch the shore for any activity Guest may get up to."

"One more thing, Brucey. We can't foresee what emergencies could arise. Especially we can't tell what could occur during the days after we return from the cave. So I'd better ask Maurice for holiday-time off – a clear four days or even a week if possible."

"That's good, laddy. Will Maurice wear it, though? From the twenty third of September, our day of action?"

"He won't like it, but I can say I'm helping you out of a fix and want time off to be with you."

"No. No, leave me out of it."

"I can manage something. Leave it to me. Meanwhile we'll carry out our guide-plan and meet at the shelter – unseen, remember – at noon on the twenty third – keeping well out of sight of anybody."

Brucey said goodnight and rang off. He was unaware that his young friend had been so intimate with Manon. Later on Leander's deceitfulness was to prove a fatal error.

XII

Friday turned out to be a scorcher. Harry wakened early, feeling eager and expectant on the morning of his meeting with Manon. Slipping into his swimming trunks, he pulled on his shorts and shirt over the top. With no more delay he went briskly to the shore and swam in the sea, careful of the current's drag. Afterwards he walked over to Eastern Cove until he came to the steep path, a mile further on, where a white sign bore the notice in red letters "DANGER Footpath unsafe." Ignoring the warning, he set off to climb down. Near the bottom the path had fallen away, but it was possible to use a protruding rock, between the fractured sections of the path, as a means of stepping across the hazard, above a fifty foot drop. Harry clambered over the gap and eventually down to the beach, a lonely and deserted part of the shore. As he reached the sand, he was surprised to see the slim figure of a girl making her way from the East towards where he stood. She was wearing a pink shirt and white shorts with unusually large turn-ups, which had the effect of drawing the eye to her shapely, brown legs.

As he walked in her direction, he recognised Manon and waved. She responded with a slight lifting of one hand.

He called out, "Hello. You're jolly early."

"What about you?" she replied.

As they met, they halted, and then each became aware of an unexpected stiffness in the other.

Manon said, "What a lovely morning."

Harry agreed. "Yes, the sun is really hot for September."

Simultaneously they began to walk westwards along the edge of the water, as it splashed in gentle swirls on the smooth, golden sand. They remained silent for a while until Manon spoke.

"You're not going to like me," she said.

Harry looked sideways at her, but he could see no more than a faint smile on her face.

"What on earth do you mean?" he asked.

"I mean I've been…", she hesitated so long that Harry could not help himself asking. "You say you have been – what have you been?"

She kicked up a spray of sand. "I wanted to tell you I've behaved badly to you. I've let you down and I don't know why."

Harry smiled encouragingly as she broke off.

"Tell me," he said. "You can't stop now, and it can't be all that bad…"

"It is to me," she interrupted. "It's about Leander. You know that Leander worked on our farm throughout the war – and afterwards too."

Harry said, "Yes."

"Well, Leander and I have been friends for a long time, since before the war. He's a nice boy but he's never quite grown up. He's awfully moody of course but we've always got on well. I was quite young when we first met. We used to play games in our imagination. You know, make up stories and imagine ourselves in another world which we invented. Until we often forgot which we were really in. Do you know what I mean?"

144

Harry nodded.

"This is where you won't like me anymore," she said.

Harry stopped but Manon kept walking and waved her hand for him to catch up. As he strode up, she said, "I eavesdropped in The Ship. I heard all you said to Alex about the letter you found, the one written by the first Leander Penhalion."

As they continued walking together, Harry felt both shocked and – he could not at first understand why – somehow also excited by this totally unexpected confidence. He did not want to say anything in case he broke the flow of her confession.

She glanced at him as if disappointed that he had not commented, and then he said, "Is that all?"

She smiled. "No. That's only the beginning."

"What next?"

She seemed encouraged by his uncritical reaction.

"When I thought I had heard enough, I decided to leave the pub before you could realise that somebody was in the bar next to you, but unfortunately in my haste I knocked over my glass. Your heard that?"

"Yes."

"I thought you would try to see who it was, and so I ran round the corner. There's a path between tall hedges leading away from the square, beside the neighbouring cottages with a small green at the back. An ancient, wooden seat stands by the grass and I ran and sat there. Yours was the only car in the park, so I waited until I heard you drive off, then I went back into the pub and rang Leander on the pay 'phone in the corridor. He got so excited when he heard what I told him, and he said he would see what his friend Brucey had to say about it. I had not met Brucey then, so I only knew of him as a specialist in antiquarian books and antiques. Leander was going to 'phone him right away. It was a thrill too, hearing of the visit to a cave on the twenty third and also the words you quoted 'a supreme example of the goldsmith's art', wasn't it?"

"Yes," Harry agreed and, as he remembered that Parkinson had 'phoned, wanting to speak to Leander that night, he asked, "and did they speak on the 'phone?"

"They played box and cox, each missing the other. But, yes, they found each other – and you saw the first result at the Lavington dance. That awful man came down – Brucey." She spoke his name with exaggerated distaste.

"Any more?" asked Harry.

"The worst," she replied. "As far as my confidences with Leander went, I was just extending my growing up days without thinking, I suppose. We'd always had that sort of relationship. It was quite natural. But I'm sorry, Harry. When you gave me the lift…"

"I know," Harry said firmly. "You don't have to tell me. I wasn't quite sure, but I thought you might have opened the cubby hole."

"I did. I couldn't see the words on the old sheets too well, but I got the details about Cellini and I saw there were careful directions where to find it in the centre of the rock platform in the cave."

"You were quick-witted in that situation, trying to read and watching out for me to return, all at the same time."

"Quick-witted maybe, but I was a heel. I'm sorry, Harry."

They had gradually come to a standstill at the water's edge.

"What else do you know?" Harry asked.

"Nothing. Except that I hate that man Brucey. I can't think what Leander can possibly see in him."

"You heard me telling Alex about the first Leander's letter. Did you know I drafted out a modern version of it – a convenient, legible copy?"

She looked puzzled. "No. Why? Should I know?"

146

"No, I just wondered. The copy letter was stolen from my bedroom."

"What! That crazy boy. It's just what I'd expect Leander to do – at Brucey's suggestion of course."

"Did Leander tell you what Brucey had to say about the treasure itself?"

"He was beside himself. He saw it as a potential fortune."

"Did Brucey find the cave?"

"I don't think so. I never heard that."

Harry stood, holding her steady gaze.

"It wasn't so bad, was it?"

Changing the subject, he added, "You know Manon, I was very fond of your mother – despite the fact that I only spoke to her on one short evening and one short morning."

"Everybody was."

"It was such a time ago too, 1938, but she made a deep impression on me."

"I'm glad."

"Thinking back, I was struck by the way your mother seemed none too happy about your boy-friends and Leander in particular."

"What a memory you have! But you're quite right. I'd been meeting Leander secretly as Mum didn't really approve of us getting together."

"Why not?"

"She understood Leander only too well. She thought that he was the kind of person who bends as circumstances change and follows whatever is said, rather than giving a lead. She always wanted to see me safely married, even at that age!" She laughed at herself. "She wanted me married off to a strong man who would look after me and keep me in order!"

"Is that what you want?" asked Harry.

"I've never thought of marriage. Well, just once. A sub-mariner, but one day his submarine never returned.

In those days I met so many men – as we all did in the WRENS – it was a new world for me, the outside world, full of people when I'd been used to a tiny circle of friends – and the wild countryside around the farm. And I'm not thinking of marriage now." She crinkled the corners of her eyes, as he remembered on another occasion, before she asked, "And you?"

"No. We've all been busy in the last six years," he replied, "with so much else."

As they walked she went on, "And what do you say? You haven't said anything. Are you cross with me?"

His answer came at once. "No. I admire your frankness. And we've all played fantasy games."

He wondered what she would have said if she had known that, not only had he watched her with Leander in the next bedroom to his at the Red House, but that he had also seen her with him yesterday evening in Lavington. What he said was, "And you tell me something. How did you get here at this hour?" He glanced at his watch. "It's only quarter to eight now – and you've been right along Eastern Cove somewhere. How did you do it?"

She started to run and shouted over her shoulder, "On my broomstick."

"You're not a witch!" he called as he ran after her.

"I got a lift from Maurice. He had to be up early to see some food suppliers, and he let me off – as he did on the day you gave me a lift. I've left my bicycle on Western Cove beach. Incidentally I brought hard-boiled eggs, lots of sandwiches and plenty of coffee for us in the saddle-bag – enough for elevenses and lunch. Then I simply walked down to the Stegenny Steps and was making my way back to the half-way path, when I saw you."

"But, it's three miles - I've seen it on the map – to the Stegenny Steps, and the half-way path is dangerous. Do you know about the break in the middle?"

"You've just come down the path. As you know it's easy if you're careful," she said. "What about trying it again. Unless you want a six mile walk via the Steps."

They returned to Red Bluff, using the half-way path, and descended the slope beyond down to the beach in Western Cove, where they sat on the turf above the sand and watched the blue sea as they soaked up the hot sunshine. There was no breeze now.

"It's hot," said Manon.

"It's perfect."

"Do you know the rock pool?"

"Yes, of course. Have you been in there?"

"Oh, yes, it's super."

"What about a swim?"

"I've got no costume."

"I'm wearing my wet trunks under these shorts. I had a swim in the sea before we met."

"Come on then."

They rose to their feet and Manon led the way over the sands to the outcrop of rocks alongside Red Bluff at the sea end. They jumped across the boulders until the sea was splashing on their right. As they climbed to the slight spur in front, they could see the curious, rock barrier which concealed the pool from the beach. Waves from the sea were breaking into thin spray which fell out of sight beyond.

When they were close to the pool, Harry called out to Manon, who was walking ahead, "I'll change."

She waved and wandered lazily over the top of the rocks until she disappeared from view.

Harry undressed to his bathing trunks and then stepped cautiously on bare feet over the hot surface of the rocks. As he put one foot carefully down on to the far side of the rock wall, he caught sight of Manon. She was standing in the sun, her clothes discarded. With the deep, blue sea and the vivid, blue sky acting together as a natural screen behind her, she looked like a beautiful naiad. She had her back to him as she balanced on the uneven edge, preparing to dive. He stared at her slim body, small waist, plump hips and long legs, the latter set apart. She leaned forwards and he saw the slight tremor of muscles before she plunged, vanishing momentarily in a seething froth of water.

Immediately he followed, diving from above and over the rocks, surfacing and thrusting across the pool with powerful crawl strokes. As he reached her, Manon let out a scream. For a minute there was laughter, when she resisted as he tried to clasp her. Then there was silence, disturbed only by the slap of breaking sea water against the end rocks.

XIII

On the 23rd September, the weather changed and, although the sun shone, it was cooler. In the bay a squall set the waves rumpling the surface of the water and skimming white spray from the sea.

At the Red House early that morning Harry had a long talk with Alex over coffee, sitting in the open on the terrace, where they were sheltered from the strong wind, and where they could discuss their plans alone together.

Alex was not going to stop Harry from rowing out to the cave if that was what he was determined to do, but she held to her view. "I think it is taking an unnecessary risk, and I wish you would be sensible and change your mind."

Whilst admitting the dangers, Harry thought that they were limited and, in any case, he was confident that he could cope with them. When the time came for them to part, they were both in an eager and relaxed mood, and they kissed. Alex called after him, "Look after yourself, Harry."

Bruce Parkinson's plan was straightforward. It was agreed between them that Leander would ensure that the shed by the sea, in the undergrowth on the shore below Red Bluff, was fully stocked up with necessary provisions for their short stay. They expected Harry Guest to make his attempt to reach the cave during the day. Meanwhile, in the event of any change in Harry's plans, or in an emergency, they were ready to remain in the cramped and uncomfortable conditions until the successful end of their mission. One of Leander's duties was to make sure that their outboard motor, for clamping on the pursuit dinghy, was in reliable, working order. They had been fortunate to trace and buy the pre-war engine from a Thames waterman whom Parkinson knew, and it had been satisfactory when they had tested it at the time.

On the 22nd September, Parkinson travelled by the overnight train to St. Aubyn and then by the Lavington and District 'bus, getting off at the Western Cove stop. There he walked across the fields by the public footpath, which joins the track from the hairpin bend and emerges opposite the point, where the undergrowth sprawls down to the shed. They were due to meet at the shed at twelve noon. Leander had estimated that this would give them plenty of time, according to the deadline printed in the local Tides Chart which he had bought. Like Harry Guest, Parkinson brought with him a haversack, containing crowbar and torch. However, unknown to Leander, he had also purchased an ex-U.S. army, automatic pistol and ammunition from one of his crooked East End contacts. He had tried slipping it into one of the pockets of his khaki canvas trousers, obtained from an army surplus store, and it fitted unobtrusively.

On the morning of the awaited day, everything went according to plan. Parkinson and Leander, preferring not to be seen together in public, made their separate ways to the shed by the shore. They greeted each other at the shed with excessive enthusiasm, revealing the relief which each felt that there had been no unexpected hold-ups. Leander had tested the outboard motor, which was ready to be carried to the dinghy and to be clipped in place on the stern. From then on they took it in turns to keep an eye on the beach, constantly watching through binoculars. Leander had provided sandwiches and hot, sweet coffee in a thermos flask, and after his overnight journey, Parkinson was first to have lunch. He was wearing his khaki trousers and a thick, white sweater; the latter garment helped to conceal the slight bulge of the slim, American pistol and he pulled the bottom of the sweater well down over his hips. On his head was a woollen hat and on his feet were blue, canvas shoes. Leander wore blue slacks and a blue, polo-necked sweater with black gumboots.

On the occasion of their last telephone conversation, Leander had pleaded with Parkinson not to have anything to drink before their trip out to the cave. Rather huffily Parkinson had agreed. But now, as he sat back from the observation window, eating his meal, he surreptitiously drank the contents of a flask, which he dragged from his hip pocket.

Parkinson had not discussed with Leander what action was to be taken, when they encountered Guest in the cave. On the only occasion that Leander had tried to raise the matter, Parkinson had said, firmly, "Leave it to me, laddy."

"Hello, there," said Harry. "Where have you come from?"

An amiable Jack Russell terrier looked up at him and wagged his tail. Harry stroked the top of the little dog's head and asked, "Where's your master? What are you doing on your own?"

The dog was small even for his breed and his markings were eccentric, a large black spot covered his left eye and the rest of his otherwise white coat was speckled with pale, brown blotches. Harry picked up a piece of driftwood and threw it into the wind. Although the dog chased after it, he soon lost sight of the wood.

"Hey, Spot!" shouted Harry pointing to his right. "Over there."

Spot took no notice, but ran up to him barking. Harry walked down to the tide line which he noticed was, as expected, unusually low and picked up the piece of wood.

"I'm busy!" he called out. "This is my last throw."

It was the chosen day for the cave. The predicted wind was blowing strongly and vapourish clouds whisked across the sky at a steady rate. It was a wild, beautiful day and the sea reflected the remorseless wind's stirring of the white-capped waves as they streamed over the surface of the water as far as the eye could see. The time had come to move. Since new clothes were still not readily available in the shops, after the wartime years of rationing, Harry was wearing his old, school games kit. He had changed after an early meal and had gone straight to the beach. With him he had brought his frayed satchel containing a commercial torch with powerful beam. It was a solid, pre-war model which he managed to buy, together with a crowbar, at a back-street ironmonger in St. Aubyn. Wrapping the crowbar in cloth, he had packed it alongside the torch. So, now he was ready.

He was about to begin winding the dinghy Jill down to the sand, when he saw the life-jacket, which he had also brought from the Red House, lying where he had dropped it.

"I mustn't forget that," he said aloud. "Alex would never forgive me." He bent forward and snatched it up into the boat with the satchel. Then he leaned on the stern of the dinghy, turned the winding wheel and lowered the boat. Detaching the cable, he paused to gaze at the blue-green sea and the frothing rim along the edge of the shore. Next he pulled the dinghy into the shallow waters of the receding tide. Leaning on the tow rope, which he had placed over his shoulder, he floated the dinghy. When he grabbed the boat and drew it towards him, he was exasperated to find that Spot was swimming alongside.

Part 3: Return to Cornwall: September 1946

"Oh, no!" he exclaimed. "Be a good dog. You must go back." He began to get anxious. The dog could wreck the whole enterprise. The time-table although vague was a tight one; and he could not afford to lose much more time. It was just after 5.00 p.m. He had allowed half an hour to reach the cave, but he wanted, if possible to have time in hand in case of difficulties at the cave mouth. It was a matter of getting the balance right; he did not want to be hanging about under the lea of Red Bluff waiting for the tide to expose the cave.

He decided that he must return the dog to the beach and hope to leave him there. If that did not work, he would have no alternative but to let the dog swim after him – and hope he would give up. He could not take him. In the turbulent conditions at the mouth of the cave, it could be dangerous to have a strange dog loose in the boat – and worse inside the cave.

Leaving the boat to drift, he seized Spot from the water and strode through the sea to the shore, where he pushed the dog away, shouting, "Go home, Spot! Home, boy!"

Spot wore a puzzled expression and his head moved expectantly in a querying way. He sat, silent. Taking the moment as time for action Harry about-faced and stalked into the sea, plunging after several yards out to the boat, where he swung effortlessly up and on to the seat. Looking back he was relieved to see that Spot was already sniffing frantically back across the foreshore, his nose close to the sand until he disappeared from sight into the undergrowth above the shore line.

Harry put on his life-jacket, picked up the oars and looked at his watch. He was running four minutes late. He hoped to make up time on the way to Red Bluff point, as he planned to enter the cave, according to the tidal chart, at a little after 5.30 p.m. It was a fairly rough pull out but the tough part was going to be at the head of the Bluff, where he could begin to row to the East. As he rowed he saw the Bluff gradually passing on his right and he scanned the beach to see if there was anybody about. He could see nothing moving on the shore, nor was there anyone visible in the grassland. He continued the steady rowing pace, pulling strongly as the head of Red Bluff towered out of the sea beside him.

Alex had naturally been disappointed not to join Harry, but she was altogether too much involved in helping her mother with the family's guests throughout the day. Previously she had gone over their plan with him; and really the issue was simple, they had synchronised their watches and estimated his return time to the Red House to be before 7.00 p.m. If he was not back after half an hour, she was to raise the alarm. They agreed in the latter event that she should contact Vivian in the first place, and if he was not to hand, she would have to find Dan and they would together see if Harry had by then arrived back on the beach. To call for assistance from anyone outside the family would be left as the last option, if no member of the family could be found.

Rowing without strain, Harry saw that the dinghy was well clear of the Bluff, so he eased the boat round, ready for the choppy haul which lay across the headland. It proved to be a gruelling row, but as he approached the dark cliff, he was able to assess that he was very near to the cave's estimated position. Concentrating on finding the site of the cave, as the boat rose and dipped, he eased it towards the fiercesome cliff, and as he rowed more strongly, he suddenly saw the opening. The cave was there, as he had remembered it, a small aperture only, but absolutely definite, a clear opening. He continued rowing. The great wall of rock seemed to be right next to him and very black, although he was still some way out. He could hear the thud of waves breaking against the neighbouring rocks. Now he was much closer. Glancing back he rowed, bobbing on the waves as he brought the dinghy across the front of the flat, rock shelf and closed in to examine it. The shelf appeared to jut out into the sea, dipping gradually and thus forming a kind of run-way, on which he judged that it would be safe to attempt to land the boat. He could see that there was an area extending outwards for several yards immediately beyond the cave, which was completely exposed and above water at present, although the breaking waves kept the surface soaking wet.

Changing course and not doubting his judgement, as he looked repeatedly over his shoulder, he calculated that the moment had come to pull the boat onto the apron of rock. The dinghy accelerated; the waves lifted it; and, whooshing backwards, the boat slid on to the flat rocks with a bang. He drew in the oars and clambered out of the boat, which was lying clear of the sea. Waves were splashing over him and over the boat, but in a few seconds it was done. One strong push and the dinghy slipped to the back of the shelf.

As he happened to glance upwards, he noticed an alcove, situated higher up on the rocks to the left of the cave. After a minute's consideration, he decided that the alcove was an altogether better place to leave Jill than, as he had planned, inside the cave; the dinghy would not only be concealed from view from the sea, but she would also be better protected, in due course, against the incoming tide. He had found the row out exhilarating rather than exhausting and he at once dragged the boat laboriously along a groove in the rocks, leading in a gentle slope from the shelf in front of the cave entrance, up to the alcove. Then he looked down at the opening. He saw that it was quite small, less than six feet high. It appeared to be wider than it actually was, because the arch to the entrance spanned some fifteen feet, although the aperture at each end was no more than a couple of feet above the base rock. Harry checked his watch; there was only twenty minutes, as estimated, in which to search the cave.

Picking up the satchel, he removed the torch and tried it out, fearful that it could have been damaged by the salt water which had splashed into the boat, but the lamp flashed out a full beam into the cave. Beyond the small entrance, which admitted inadequate daylight, was a cavernous interior, reaching up to twenty and thirty feet according to the variable surface of the roof. Harry shone the beam slowly round, noticing every detail, as he observed all he could before starting his search for the cavity hiding place. It was a strange scene. The floor of the cave was pitted with small pools of seawater of various depths, but otherwise it was even, broken for part of its length by a diagonal running rib of rock from one corner to the other, covering about twenty five yards altogether. As the Leander letter had described, the back of the cave was a remarkable raised platform measuring perhaps fifteen feet across and – as he shortly discovered – it was situated at a regular distance from the rear wall, forming a long crevice; and at one end there was a natural ramp at an angle of about forty five degrees from the floor of the cave to the top of the theatrical platform, at a height of fifteen feet.

Harry shone the light from the torch generally round the semi-circle of the cave, lighting up the junction of the cave floor to the cave wall. He walked to the end of the platform, where he turned and before returning swung the beam onto the back of the platform. Moving closer, he aimed the beam of the torch into the crevice itself, and saw that it looked to be about two feet deep. The crevice ended at the commencement of the ramp, where it joined the rear wall of the cave. According to the letter, he had to start his search at the middle point of the crevice. The back wall of the crevice which actually faced the rear wall of the platform – and was therefore for the main part out of sight – could only be reached, as he knew from the letter's directions, by lying down on the platform and feeling along the hidden nearside of the crevice. Realising that his life-jacket would hinder him, he removed it.

The cave was filled with the roar and smack of the sea breaking on the rocks beyond the entrance and the moaning of the wind in the narrow opening. He listened to the incessant sounds and looked at the cave's entrance when, for an instant, he thought he detected a scraping sound. It was an eerie place. Shortly after, re-assured by the continual movement of the sea and the whining wind, he lay face down and began to search, shining the torch ahead, not easy in the confined space available. In fact his back became cramped in the awkward position. As a result of this he started getting to his feet to stretch himself. When he reached a crouching position, he was holding out the torch in front of him with the light switched off so as to conserve the battery. However, before he could stand erect, he was struck from behind by a glancing blow to the back of his head.

Harry dropped, unconscious, onto the rock platform. His lamp disappeared from sight into the crevice with a loud crack.

XIV

After Harry's collapse onto the rock platform inside the cave beneath Red Bluff, it was a long time before he revived.

But now he was standing uncertainly in semi-darkness, dazed and bewildered as the green water splashed below him in the cave. Then while he watched the swirling water lapping the rock edge, he noticed a change in the flow. The light coming from outside the cave had been reduced because the rising water had, as it covered the entrance, blocked the way. In addition, the sound of the sea-water's turmoil had lessened. Whilst high tide must still be hours away, yet surely the water had a long way to rise before it reached anywhere near to the platform where he stood. Excitement at this knowledge jolted his hazy memory and shifted his mood from despair to hope. He only had to wait for the tide to turn. Then he remembered Alex. She would be waiting for him, anxious about their agreed deadline as it came closer.

Yes, it was absolutely clear. Despite the conditions which he imagined he would have to face outside the cave – powerful cross currents, a heavy sea, underwater rocks and a long swim to the shore down the West side of the headland – he really had no alternative. He must swim underwater from the cave to the sea and back to the beach.

Must watch out for the jagged rocks over the cave entrance and then swim steadily for the shore. Hope my head's up to it. It must be. Anyhow, I'm sure of one thing: I must have slipped on wet rocks and knocked myself out. Back of my head must have struck the granite platform. Stupid of me. Let's get on now. Best to keep my plimsolls with me – need them on the beach. So, I'll take them off and tie them together by the laces. Loop them over my belt at the back. Leave on my shirt and shorts. Maybe the sea will drag off my socks but they will help protect my feet until I'm clear of the sharp rocks.

He lowered himself into the water and swam towards the ghostly light at the opening of the pool, below water. Taking a deep breath, he ducked under water and swam strongly downwards, managing to avoid the rocky archway. He swam for as long as he could holding his breath, and when he surfaced, gasping, he found himself well clear of the rocks.

Outside it was twilight. Red Bluff looked black and grim against the darkening sky above, towering on guard over the agitated sea. The combination of cold water and strong wind gave him an unexpected uplift as he set off swimming with a steady crawl stroke towards the end of the headland. On reaching his first objective, he knew he must pull firmly away from the area of the cave, to clear the unruly currents.

As he rounded the Bluff, he could see the early evening lights from scattered homes, high above the bay, and then he settled to a determined swim for the shore. But shock and his over-stretched efforts were taking a toll, as he persevered in the black water. Once when he tried resting by treading water, he grew anxious as the current dragged him out towards the open sea. Briskly he reverted to the crawl, gradually progressing beside the headland until he heard, louder and closer, the waves breaking on the beach. Soon the rollers swamped him in a rhythmic movement, and the tide took over and cast him in a heap on the sands. When he pulled himself free from the hammering waves, he lay still for what seemed an interminable time as twilight changed to early night.

At last he stood on bare feet and noticed that his socks had been torn off during the swim. He walked erratically for a few steps up the beach until he came to a familiar sign "DANGER. No Swimming" and to the rocks where the two Red House dinghies were berthed, safely together on the shelf above the sand, winched up and secured to tarred timbers. Although it was getting dark now, Harry could see the shape of the two boats, lying side by side in their usual places. Two boats! For a moment he stood, uncomprehending. That's impossible. As he stared, his memory became clearer. In the moments of panic as he recovered in the cave, all thought of the existence of the boats had been blocked from his mind, while he concentrated all his efforts on getting away. But, two dinghies. Of course. I remember launching one of them. In fact I rowed it out thisafternoon. I landed it – and dragged the boat under cover. Into a rocky alcove above. Yet here is the boat back by the shore. Impossible. What's happened? I can hardly believe my eyes.

But, then, like an exploding firework inside his head, he saw the answer to the conundrum. Somebody had recovered the dinghy and brought it back from outside the cave. It's part of a carefully laid plan. Somebody meant to deprive me of the means of escape from the cave. Somebody also hoped to confuse any search party which might be mounted to look for me later on. I took out the boat Jill. But Jill is beside her companion Jack – complete evidence to the outside world that, apparently, I never put to sea. Only Alex knew that I intended trying to reach the cave this evening using the dinghy Jill. But, faced with this incontrovertible proof, as it would seem, that the two boats had never left their berths, what would she think?

Damn, I've got a splitting headache. Never mind. Let's sort it all out. Who attacked me? I know that I never fell accidentally; after seeing the boats, that is. Brucey must be responsible. Yet is Brucey really capable of such a ruthless crime? Leaving somebody alone and helpless to drown in the cave when the tide swept in? Leander? Not possible. But, someone, under cover of the noise of breaking waves – must have crept up on me. Felled me with a single blow and left me to drown. Brucey. It looks as if it was Brucey. True, Brucey had a powerful motive. He must have read the stolen copy letter pages, and so he knew the potential value of the prize contents which might be lying in the cave. But did Brucey have the guts to carry out such a crime?

Harry stretched out on the sand to recover in the dark, and promptly dropped off into a fitful sleep which slipped into a nightmare world where he found himself struggling for life under water with a multi-tentacled sea monster. The creature's hot, panting breath warmed his cheeks. But on opening his eyes, he saw a writhing shape close to his head; confused, he jerked away in panic at the unknown, and then, hearing a high pitched bark, fell back on the sand. Spot had discovered him on the shore and was licking his face.

The little dog leaned against his shoulder.

"Good old Spot!" said Harry, putting out his hand to stroke the dog. The movement disturbed his plimsolls which were still hanging from his belt, so he removed them and slipped them on to his feet.

He spoke softly to Spot again, and while his hand played with Spot's ear, he caught sight of the luminous dial of his watch. He recalled buying it in 1942 in Cairo while he was on short leave from the desert – from "up the blue" as it was called. He had first seen the watch suspended by its stainless steel strap in a fish tank filled with water. The tank had been the centrepiece of a luxury shop window, where it demonstrated that the watch was waterproof. The large, second hand could be seen sweeping round the watch face in its submerged case. He had never seen a waterproof watch before the war, and bought it at once, because only such a watch could keep out the all-penetrating desert sands.

He had forgotten all about the time. His watch showed 7.20 p.m. Help! I must return to Alex before the emergency plan is due. It's got colder. He shivered in the blustering wind and heard the waves breaking nearby.

"Come on, Spot!" he said, crossing the sand, but quickly halting to clasp his right hand to his forehead as he felt a painful spike from the wound. Spot was soon back to find out the reason for the delay.

The night was not pitch black, because the sky was brilliant with stars and a pale moon so that he could see the outline of the dinghies. Before leaving the shore he clambered carefully over the rocks and grasped the stern of the small boat Jill, lying on the shelf above the sand, as if to convince himself that it was really there. As he held the woodwork, he saw a glint reflected from the moon, in the darkness at the bottom of the boat. He must have seen it from a particular angle, for however he stood, he could not pick it out again with his eyes. Leaning over the side of the boat, he felt about among the duckboards fitted inside, but his fingers contacted nothing. He stood up and at once caught sight of a momentary light as if from a metal surface. This time he stretched out his hand to the point where he had seen the flash, and grasped an object which was lying obliquely beneath the seats. It was a watch on a leather strap, which had worn through. He put it into the breast pocket of his shirt.

Harry noticed that Spot had moved to the boat with him and was sitting hard on his foot.

"Right, boy. Let's go."

Part 3: Return to Cornwall: September 1946

Walking with stiff footsteps, to protect his head, he stepped down from the rocks to the sand and then on to the firm ground of the path, and mounted the incline which eventually led to the Red House. As he climbed upwards cautiously, he asked himself, what am I going to tell Alex?

Several steps later he decided. He would remain quiet for the time being. He would tell Alex that he slipped in the cave and fell on the rocks, hurting the back of his head. He would also withhold the subsequent facts; he would not tell her that he swam from the cave to the shore; nor that he walked back up the beach and was stunned to see the dinghy Jill somehow returned to her berth. Perhaps, much later.

Ahead of him loomed the Red House as he climbed the winding path leading to the steps up to the forecourt. Spot, who was still in front of him, scampered back and jumped up, placing his front paws against Harry's legs. It was as if he was saying goodbye, because he doubled up the steps afterwards and disappeared.

Harry did not want to be noticed in his soaking clothes, so he entered the house by the back door and hastily borrowed Vivian's duffle coat which was hanging on the wall. It was lucky that, as he was buckling up the coat's last toggle, Alex came into the hall.

"Harry!"

"Alex, can you come upstairs a minute?"

"How did you get on? I was beginning to worry."

"No luck, I'm afraid. I slipped on the rocks and bumped the back of my head."

"Let me see," she said. "Oh! Nasty!"

She had no doubt what must be done. She immediately picked up the telephone and called the family doctor. She spoke briefly.

"We're going at once," she explained as she returned the black 'phone to its cradle. "The doctor will see you in the surgery in ten minutes."

Harry said, "I'll change first."

"No, come as you are. The sooner we get your head seen to the better," she insisted and opened the living room door to call out to her father that she was borrowing the car, but did not expect to be long.

As they left the drive, Harry told Alex about the dog which he called Spot.

"It must be Phil Tregoran's dog," she said. "His dog's got a black patch on one eye, but he calls him Patch. His father, Bill, looks after Patch when Phil's at sea. You remember them, don't you?"

Alex was a good driver. She drove to Lavington at speed. When they reached the town, she braked as she entered the square. She was nearing the sharp, left hand turning on the far side, when she changed gear and slowed to a crawl, the headlights picking out the solid, corner stones of the houses on the other side of the road. The lights dappled the stone walls, mingling with the headlights of a car approaching from the opposite direction. She saw that it was likewise slowing down for the corner. Harry noticed the full beam of the on-coming car's headlights as they filled the road in between. Alex flashed her headlights to remind the driver that the car's lights were undipped but the other headlights stayed full on. In consequence Alex was concentrating too hard on negotiating the awkward corner to notice who the car's occupants were. However, from where Harry was sitting, he could see both the driver and the passenger of the car, and he felt the back of his neck prickle. At the same moment the driver of the car recognised Harry. It was Parkinson with Leander at his side. Harry had never before seen anybody look so alarmed and incredulous.

Alex completed the turn while Harry stretched his head behind to observe the other car's progress. As he watched, the car swerved as Parkinson desperately tried to avoid a parked car on his near side, but he was too late. The brake lights flashed crimson in the night, and Harry could not help smiling as he heard a dull crash of the collision with the parked car.

"What was that?" asked Alex who had not seen the accident in the rear mirror.

"The car we passed hit another one parked by the side of the road."

"Should we stop?"

"No – nothing to do with your driving. And the car was going so slowly that nobody could have been hurt." He would not tell her now who was in the car. He would leave that until much later.

The doctor was standing on the doorstep of his house, the light shining behind him as the car drew in. He examined Harry's wound in the surgery, bathed and dressed it and declared, "You're lucky. The wound is clean, but it will need regular dressings. I'll give you something to put on it. Gently mind – Alex will help you. Change daily and see how it goes. But, you'll need to take it easy. Rest. Come back – if you're staying down here – or get it seen by your own doctor – in a week's time. And beforehand if you feel unwell. Don't delay. That's important. You've had a hard crack there."

When the pair returned, the Penhalions were full of sympathy on learning of Harry's fall. Their party was nearing a close, their guests relaxing over CampCoffee before departing. Jean came out to the hall to answer the telephone as it began to ring.

Jean's expression changed as she spoke.

"But why? Why so suddenly?" she asked.

The caller continued speaking.

"Well," said Jean with a steely edge to her voice which Harry had never heard before. "I think it's absurd, but if that's what you've planned to do, Leander, I suppose that's that. Thank you for letting us know."

She put the 'phone down, looking about her, exasperated.

"You heard, Alex? Leander! Oh, what an infuriating boy! What do you think he's up to now?"

"What?" asked Alex, alarmed.

Jean shook her head. "No, nothing to be worried about, or at least I don't think so. But he's left. He's off by the overnight train from St. Aubyn. Apparently he's had an urgent call from Brucey, and he says he must join him in London. He wants to help Brucey out."

At this point Harry said he was going to bed. Jean and Alex wanted to know if he needed anything, but thanking them, he said, "No, I just need a good night's sleep. Goodnight."

As he climbed the stairs, taking each step carefully so as to protect his head, he considered the significance of Leander's 'phone call to his mother. Leander's run away from Cornwall. He's hiding his head in the ground, ostrich fashion. And he hasn't told his mother that Brucey is with him. Just a lie about a call from Brucey in London. They are together. They must be trying to avoid any trouble after attacking me in the cave. But why? There's no evidence that they ever went to the cave. There's nothing I can prove. What can they be up to? On second thoughts, I don't believe they would leave Cornwall now and go to London, even if they wanted to lie low. And they must want the Masterpiece! – however incomprehensible their actions have been so far. What, then, are they really up to? I half thought they could have used the concealed shed by the shore in their original plans. Leander would have known all about it from childhood days, and he might well have suggested it to Brucey as a perfect hideout. So, perhaps they used it as a look-out to establish exactly when I set out for the cave. And they must also have worked out a speedy way to catch up with me. What about an outboard engine for the dinghy, Jack? Something like that would explain everything. If I'm right, they would know, in the present emergency, to carry on using the shed so as to be certain of keeping a close eye on what my next move was going to be. They must be staying there, and they have probably stocked up with food and water and so on.

When he reached his bedroom, Harry took off the duffle coat and immediately noticed the lump in his shirt pocket. Pulling out the watch, which he had found in the dinghy, he looked at it closely. It was a simple watch with "Helvetia" printed on the centre of its silver face. When he flicked it over in his hand to check the reverse side, he saw that there was an inscription on the backplate. Holding the watch up to the light, he read the following:

"To L. from G., 1935.
O, thou art fairer
than the evening air."

To fit the minute space available, the engraver had set the words into three lines, splitting the single line quotation into two, separate lines. Harry took the letter 'L' to stand for Leander and 'G' for Geoffrey and '1935' was probably the year, when the two had met for the first time. What a queer pair they are, he thought.

Weary and with a throbbing head, Harry was thankful to undress and get into bed, where he lay still, his mind at first too full for sleep. When he did eventually sleep, he was trying to puzzle out which poet had written the line of verse, which was engraved on the back of the watch. In the morning, after a long and blissful night's rest, he wakened late and found that, instead of concentrating, as might have been expected, on yesterday's amazing events, he was still wondering which poet had composed the words of the inscription. Opening his eyes, he noticed the small shelf of books against the wall near the window, where he recalled on a previous occasion he had noticed an old anthology of poetry.

He sat up too quickly and a sharp pain immediately passed through his head. Getting out of bed with care, he reached for the anthology from the shelf. He instinctively opened the book at the section devoted to the poetry of Christopher Marlowe and at once came upon the well-known quotation from 'Dr. Faustus' which describes Helen of Troy.

He began to read:

"Was this the face that launch'd a thousand ships..."

– and a few lines further on he found the following:

"O, thou art fairer than the evening air
Clad in the beauty of a thousand stars!"

Substituting Leander for Helen of Troy in his mind, Harry thought, that's a bit steamy.

XV

After the momentous encounter and the minor accident in Lavington, Brucey and Leander instantly agreed to a change of their plans. They knew they must have an urgent talk about their next step in the light of the extraordinary new circumstances. Since they had already provided reasonable, if fairly limited supplies, at their hidden shelter by Western Cove, they decided to return there immediately. Preparations for the vigil to see when Harry Guest would set out for the cave, had included taking blankets for makeshift beds.

Brucey drove from Lavington to the 'bus stop situated a mile or so down the road which passed near the cove by a track leading to Red Bluff's beach.

On the way Leander said, "As you know I never told my parents that Maurice has given me several days off during our cave efforts. Good job we fixed that with him beforehand. But I shall have to explain my absence to them now."

"Why not say you're joining me in London?"

"What? Say you want my assistance urgently?"

"Yes. They won't question that. Say it's an emergency – it's true enough!"

Leander then raised the matter of where the car should be parked. "It's not safe in the trees here, in view of all that's happened. I'd be happier if I put the car by the barn in the lower entrance to the Red House. It would be a reasonable place if anybody finds it, and they'll think I got a taxi to St. Aubyn station – where I'll say I'm going."

Brucey, after driving off the road, climbed uncertainly from the car as Leander moved over into the driver's seat.

Leaning out the window, Leander said, "I'll give the Victory "V" call by rapping it out on the shelter door when I get back – the war-time Morse signal – and then I'll repeat it a second time when you can safely open up. But, please, don't put any light on till I'm inside and the door shut. Alright?"

"Yes, laddy. Get a move on. We want to keep together. You'll find me in the shelter. I've got the key."

"I won't be long."

Driving back to Lavington Leander stopped at the public telephone kiosk on the edge of the town. On the 'phone he told his mother his story about going to London. He was stung and surprised at the heat in Jean's voice as she replied. But there was nothing he could do about that. Next, he drove on to the Red House. As he approached he switched off the car lights and the engine, and let the car roll quietly downhill until he reached the second entrance, a hundred yards West of the house. The gate was open, and he steered the car in, and parked on the side of the barn away from the house. Without slamming the door, he hurried away to join Brucey at the foot of the hill. At the shelter he rapped out the signal.

It was at this point that Leander realised how shaken Brucey was. As he opened the door, Brucey exclaimed, his voice quivering with emotion at seeing the young man again, "Thank God you're back. Everything all set with the car? Nobody saw you?"

"I don't think so. But we have to be very careful how we enter and leave this hut. We don't want to attract any attention."

"Yes, yes, but you say you think you weren't seen…"

"I mean I wasn't seen. Nothing occurred, but I don't know if somebody was around in the dark. But, don't worry, Brucey. Let's brew up some really hot coffee. That's what we could both do with!"

Leander had already lighted the hurricane lamp after covering the only window with sacking and shielding the light from the door with a chair. They sat on garden chairs sipping the hot drinks, which Brucey had heated on the primus stove in the yellow lamplight.

Brucey spoke first. "Thank God we made it."

They had to talk now, compulsively. They had to go over in full detail the events as these had unfolded into the dangerous fiasco of their visit to the cave at Red Bluff point. Earlier they had both been unable to say a word, altogether too shocked by what at first sight had seemed to be an almost supernatural event in Lavington. Now they were both smarting from a mixture of fear and from uncomfortably depressing feelings of failure at the whole absurd and inept enterprise's conclusion.

Leander said, "I still can't believe it. How the hell did he do it?"

"Damn the man. And how did he manage to get out of the cave with no dinghy – in spite of being knocked out – and all so quickly?"

Leander could not disguise his admiration of the achievement. "He must have regained consciousness. And he was flat out when we dumped him on the rock ledge. And he must have swum back. He's a strong man. We're up against a cracker."

"Cracker, my foot. He's a bastard. And we'll beat him to it. But first of all we've got to look at this in minute detail and see what went wrong."

"It all came about, because I knew Manon," Leander began. "Whilst I was working at Moorland Farm, she told me what she'd overheard at The Ship when Guest and Alex were talking about the sixteenth century Leander letter and its reference to hidden gold. I rang you at once and we had difficulty getting each other on the 'phone. I know, when I finally spoke to you, I was surprised by your reaction. I thought you would be pleased, but I never expected you to be so much overboard about it, although of course I understand now."

Parkinson took up the story. "It is one of those issues which you know in your bones is important. I knew at once, on the limited facts – supported as they were, of course by your long-standing, local legend of the gold treasure – that there could be something here to make our lives a luxury: almost as if we had Faustus' cornucopia of wealth – without making any pact with Lucifer! And so I came down to Cornwall, didn't I? And we found that interfering soldier had stuck his nose into your affairs, persuading your silly sister to go along with his plan to find the Marlowe treasure. But, dear boy, he bit off more than he could chew, when I suggested that you should retrieve your family's Leander letter from that fellow's bedroom: which you achieved magnificently – at least you obtained the copy letter, or at any rate most of it."

Leander smiled. It had not been a problem. Since he occasionally went home during the day, there had been no difficulty about getting away from the farm for an hour. Once he had reached home, as a member of the family, it would always have seemed natural if he had been found in his own home during the day, but he had wanted to avoid being noticed if possible. Consequently he had been careful to choose a time when Harry was expected to be out, and everything quiet, before tea at about three thirty in the afternoon. Well prepared he had invented a story to tell in case he was seen. He would pick up one of the bathing towels which were invariably left each day to dry on the window sill. Then he would explain, if necessary, that he was returning one of Harry's towels which had fallen on the path under the window.

Leander said, "I somehow thought he would put the letter under his clothes in one of the drawers, because that's where I'd have left it if I had been in his shoes. So, I looked there first. And I was right. Unfortunately I was interrupted by the sound of footsteps on the landing. So, I grabbed a sheaf of pages of the letter in one hand and with the other picked up a bathing towel hanging on the window sill – my alibi – and then carefully opened the door. Molly, the daily help, was at the end of the corridor. I flung the towel, not needed now, towards the window and quickly slipped downstairs without being seen.

"The funny thing is that there was no family fuss afterwards as I had expected. So Guest must have decided to say nothing. Maybe he didn't tell my sister – or if he did, maybe she agreed to keep quiet about it too. After all, they both deceived the family…"

"Disgraceful, I think, as you know, laddy," interrupted Parkinson. "And so you came up to London to meet me and we talked things over and examined the extraordinary copy of Leander's letter which that man, Guest, had prepared. We wondered why he had copied it. However, later, when you reported that Manon had seen the original letter, she seemed to have the answer; the letter was very hard indeed to read in its ancient form. He would also have needed a copy for ready reference, perhaps because he had put the original in a bank for safe keeping. As things went, you kept your eye open, but nothing came up. So, we got ready for 23rd September, the date of the Autumn Equinox, as we had established. That's when we expected the soldier to row out to Red Bluff point. Manon told you she had seen him rowing one of the two Red House guests' dinghies on some previous occasion, and so it was likely that he would use one of them without drawing any particular attention to himself – as he would have done, for example, if he had hired a motor boat. So, we settled for this old, tarred, storage shed as our base in the undergrowth above the shore. It's not been used for years. You checked, and so you knew that you could get a good view of the beach from the only window in the building, in spite of the creeper growing up outside. You had played here as a boy and so you were familiar with the surroundings."

He became absorbed in his thoughts which were diverting his mind from the crisis. "We also got together all the things we'd need. You know – primus stove, a few cooking utensils plus plates, mugs, cutlery – not many – and then some tinned food, a bottle opener and some large water containers." He thought for several seconds and then continued. "Next, blankets, a couple of garden chairs, plus a spade and not forgetting toilet paper. We made sure, laddy, we had enough supplies, anyway, to cover for unexpected contingencies. And you removed the sole key of the shelter to prevent anybody entering and finding out what was going on."

Leander added, "I also picked up the outboard motor which you sent down. At St. Aubyn station. I carried it down to the shed overnight to avoid being seen with it. When the day came nearer, I tested the engine thoroughly. It was going fine and the old shed timbers would have muffled the sounds. I listened outside to check and you could hardly hear anything, not unless you were very close."

"This morning," said Parkinson, "you didn't tell your family you'd agreed with Maurice to have a few days off from Moorland Farm. But – you've squared that since with your 'phone call to your mother. However, at the time when you drove out – as you normally would do if going to the farm – you went instead by a roundabout route to the shelter, taking with you some overlooked provisions, and then waited for me, sorting out the place to make it tolerably habitable."

Leander spoke slowly as he added, "You know, there is one thing I've not considered properly before. We were lucky there was nobody about, either when we launched the boat Jack, or later when we brought back the two, Jack and Jill and winched them up to their berths. We were sensible too to take turns, at the outset, watching from the shed window. It was the perfect place with a good view. And safe – because concealed and really known only to a few people – and locked."

"I knew we had to speed to the cave. And the outboard motor we'd prepared and hidden was the answer. But, laddy, you've put your finger on a weak point. We'd have been scuppered if anyone had been around. Or, rather, we'd have been seen if anyone had been on the beach. And, as far as any sighting from the cliffs above could be concerned – as you assure me – it is impossible to see the foreshore at all from any of the buildings up there. And, it would not have been possible to identify anyone in a boat at sea from that distance, even with glasses. In due course, as Guest rowed out of sight round the Bluff, it was time to go. The little boat Jack was free, which was vital too – and, as we've said, there was nobody anywhere in sight, when we broke cover with the outboard motor and clipped it in place on the boat. Then we got the boat shifted down and into the sea in no time. Once aboard and floating on the windy water, I was pulling hard on the oars getting us out to sea, while you heaved the cord three or four times before the engine burst into life."

Leander grinned. "The landing wasn't easy, was it? And we had to be careful not to get the dinghy holed on the rocky ledge."

"Getting there wasn't easy either, in those choppy waters and under the hulking great Bluff."

"But, we did it well. I was surprised, when we arrived, because there was no sign of the other boat. Then we saw that Guest had gone to the trouble of lugging his boat up to that cleft in the rocks beside the cave. But I was even more surprised that he never seemed to hear the bang as our boat struck the flat rocks at the cave entrance."

"There was a lot of other noise, laddy, inside the cave. That's what ditched him. He never heard us. And when we got really close, and he began to stand up, pulling something with him in his right hand, I was convinced that he had discovered the treasure trove. I could have sworn that he was lifting it from the back of the crevice on the rock platform – but it turned out to be a torch he was holding."

They both fell silent.

Parkinson started to speak, but changed his mind and Leander could see from the white knuckles of his clenched fists on his knees that he was worked up.

Then Leander asked, "What made you do it, Brucey?"

Parkinson began to get angry and his face grew red. But with an effort he appeared to control his feelings. Minutes passed and Leander held Parkinson's eye as he replied.

"It was blind rage. Seeing Guest there. I believed he'd just picked up the treasure. And if he had done, it meant we'd got what we'd come for. I could therefore think of nothing else but Guest himself – isolated there in the cave – in fact laddy, I saw him as being in my power. There came to me again and again and again, repeatedly going through my head the names you told me Guest called me on the evening after the dance in Lavington – in front of all your family."

Parkinson paused, breathing heavily. When he continued, Leander had difficulty hearing his lowered voice.

"I never planned it. It was just those words driving through my head: 'bad-tempered old poofter'!"

178

He seemed to be wrestling to bring out the next words. "Something sparked off a bright flash of light behind my eyes – or so it felt to me. Nothing could have stopped me. I was beyond control. Well, as you know, we had brought along a crowbar in case we needed to prise the goods from the rocks."

His voice shook with emotion as he said, "Guest was lucky. He moved unexpectedly, at the last moment, and so he only received a glancing blow when I hit him with the crowbar."

And so it was out in the open – an unwitting movement had probably saved Harry's life. The violent assault had been provoked by those potent, contemptuous words which Brucey had only heard repeated at second-hand by Leander. In years to come in a totally different context allegations would be made that very similar words – also repeated at second-hand and as deeply offensive – were heard behind the notorious murder which took place in public at the height of gangland feuding in London's East End. Malicious words, when repeated by a third party, have the capacity to increase in invective power over the same words spoken directly face to face.

Brucey remained silent until Leander touched his friend's hand.

"Why couldn't you have said that before, Brucey? I understand and I would have felt as you did."

"Laddy, I don't know," Parkinson replied. "But the next step, inside the cave, was worse. God, how the tide changed! Suddenly – unbelievable! That's going to be the danger when we go again. No wonder your name-sake is said to have been drowned there! What speed!"

"Well, Brucey, we tried hard to drag Guest out to the boat, which he'd left next to the cave, but the waters were rushing in on us and sent us flying. We kept trying but each time the waves became stronger and stronger and more frequent and bowled us over. Finally you shouted out that we must save ourselves. I said we must leave Guest where he would have a chance of survival, and so we heaved him between us, until we were all three flung against the ramp of rock at the back of the cave where at last we pulled him to safety on the platform above."

"We wasted too much time on him," Parkinson commented. "As a result, we had the devil's own task getting away. The soldier's boat – the one named Jill – was O.K., tucked in the rift in the rocks. He knew what he was up to, shifting it to safety up there. But, the other one, Jack, was nearly wrecked, being bashed against the headland rocks at the foot of the Bluff. I tell you, we only just did it, dear boy. There was no possibility of taking Guest with us."

"Then we almost failed to launch the boats," said Leander.

"Yes. I got Jack out and it plunged like a jet away from the rocks, leaving you behind. There was no way of controlling her in that sea. I was damned lucky to get the outboard motor going quickly. I thought she would turn turtle a number of times."

"I must say I was relieved after that, when I managed to get Jill off as well. I've never been so frightened, ever before. I didn't think we would make it. And I was so relieved that you got clear, Brucey. It was a miracle that we both survived."

There was a pause in the flow of reminiscences until Parkinson continued. "But we did return safely. And we berthed the two dinghies beside the winch up on the rocks. Then we carried on to the shelter where you dumped the outboard motor. We also spruced ourselves up a bit, changing out of our wet clothes and into spares we'd got ready in store. I was really dying for a drink by this time."

Leander said, "I suggested the New Inn as a good choice for our drink. Because it's the only place in the district, where I'm not known, on the coast, beyond Western Cove. We wanted time to recover and plenty of beer to aid the process. Above all we had to work out what to do about Guest. We had to make an attempt to get him back from his resting place on the ledge inside the cave. We thought that there must be at least one more tide low enough for us to re-enter the cave for that purpose – although there was still the Cellini to find."

Parkinson spoke without enthusiasm. "We decided that we would take Jack out there on the next tide. We also agreed that we would tell Guest, when we reached him in the cave, that we had seen him row out in those wild conditions and that we had become worried, as he had failed to re-appear after a reasonable time. We would say that we had followed him and that we had come across him lying unconscious on the floor of the cave, and that we had assumed that he must have fallen on the wet rocks. We would point out that the raging, incoming tide had made it impossible to get his dead weight away, and so we had left him, safely laid out on the rock platform and had gone back to the beach. In conclusion we would declare that we had now returned by the following tide, laddy, in order to fetch him to the shore – and that's what we had come to do."

Leander said, "Ironically we were actually driving to the shelter by the seashore for our long wait until we could judge that the time and tide were right for launching Jack to rescue him. And what happens?"

There was a grim look on Parkinson's face as he recalled the meeting in the square at Lavington. He said, "And then, after that long haul back, to meet that bloody man, Guest, in the town! God's truth! I thought I'd seen a ghost."

"No wonder you drove into that parked car." Leander shuddered. He was still suffering from shock. "Well," he said, "we did the right thing, not stopping to find the car's owner after the crash. We didn't want to advertise ourselves just at that moment. And, thank Heavens, one good thing came out of it all – for me anyway. We got away from Western Cove. Together." He repeated the last word fervently. "Together."

"It was a good moment for me too, laddy – in the end."

"And we don't have the problem of bringing back Guest from the cave," Leander said, adding as an after-thought, "But what about my watch? I told you I lost it. And it has the engraving on the back of it."

"But, you don't know where you lost it. It could be in the cave, in the sea, in the sand, anywhere."

"I hope it isn't in the boat."

"Don't be a fool. Why should it be in the boat? Anyhow, that doesn't prove anything, even if you dropped it in the boat. You could have lost it, say, when you innocently leaned on the boat when passing by."

"Yes, but Guest will know we must have brought back his dinghy, Jill."

"It means nothing. There's still no proof we were anywhere near the cave. Guest never saw us either in the cave or on the beach. Don't make things worse than they are. Forget all about it. I'm sorry you lost your watch. That's all there is to be said. I'll get you another watch – when this is all over. You go to sleep. We both need it, but we must be on the job at first light. We must be ready in the morning and then take turns, as before, watching the shoreline for any movement. For anything Guest may get up to. Have you got it, laddy?"

"Yes, Brucey. Sleep well."

Shaken by recent events, Brucey's mind was not yet ready for sleep.

Plans for the morning. Best not to make a lot of detailed plans. May go wrong anyway. And, in spite of everything, much is on our side. Plenty of advantages over Guest. Outboard motor first and foremost. Even if Guest had twigged we'd got one. Meant a speedy return from the cave. And, I never told Leander. But my pistol could rule the day. Got it nicely concealed too. No need for making rules. If something goes wrong, then sort it out on the spot as we've just done. And the hidden shelter, here, was a first-class hide-away to choose. What more?

Repeating the question over and over again in his head, Brucey finally fell asleep.

XVI

Harry was not fit yet, but the long day's complete rest yesterday had been a help. Certainly, on waking in the morning, he was feeling much better and to his surprise, his head no longer ached. The wound, however, was very sore.

Alex was reluctant to allow Harry to go to the cave again, but she was helpful in gathering replacements for the various things he had left behind in the cave. First of all she produced her old school satchel. Next, she went to the Lavington Post Office shop where she was surprised to find a crowbar which had been in stock for years. She also bought a new battery for the Red House reserve torch which she offered, for him to take. So, he was well equipped.

Irrespective of Alex's previous idea of joining Harry in his attempt to enter the cave, she was again constricted because her parents were to be out and had asked her to be at home to deal with any calls.

Now Harry was standing in the bay, breathing in the fresh sea air. He hoped that the tide would allow reasonable time to explore the cave in spite of losing two days. Then, without thinking, he bounded on to the springy turf nearby and immediately grimaced at the sharp pain which spiked into the sensitive scar on his head. Despite this, he was much more like his usual self, confident and ready for whatever lay ahead that day.

Striking diagonally away from the footpath, he was careful to step gingerly onto the sand, where he looked around to reassure himself that there was nobody in sight. The seashore was deserted: no witnesses apparent. He moved up to the dinghy named Jill and flung the satchel into it before untying the boat from its upright beams. To his astonishment, while he was easing the dinghy into position, he heard a voice above the gusting wind.

"Harry! It's me!" called Manon.

He straightened up, wondering where she had come from, but he was unable to conceal his anxious expression at seeing her at this particular time.

"What's the matter? Have you got a hang-over?" She laughed at him.

"Sorry. I'm thinking about getting this thing down the slope and across the beach and into the sea," he explained.

She ignored his attempt to avoid the issue, and came to the point. "Can I come with you?"

"No. It's too rough."

She mocked him. "Only safe for a big man like you, is it?" But there was the suggestion of a smile at the corners of her mouth.

The situation, to say the least, was difficult for Harry. Was Manon going to spoil his chance of entering the cave this time? Then, it struck him that she knew all the facts about his proposed trip and its purpose, and that she may have come to the beach at this time with the deliberate intention of embarrassing him. Yet he also saw that she could have a genuine desire to join him in the venture. He thought it was best to be frank.

"Do you know what I am doing?" he asked.

"Yes, of course I do. You are going to the cave."

"In that case, why are you here on the 25th September?"

"Isn't that the day you're trying to reach the cave?"

"The day was to have been the 23rd, but I changed it for to-day."

"Oh, silly me! I'd still like to join you, please."

"In that case, keep facing me."

"I beg your pardon?" She was startled.

"It's just that my guess is that we're being observed."

"Observed?" she asked.

"Yes, I think we're being watched from the old store house. It's up to you, and I suppose it doesn't matter all that much. Except that we don't want to precipitate a crisis at this stage. It could stop us from launching the boat – and it's vital that we keep to my time table, if we're to have even a small chance of success. Everything depends on the tide and our timing. And with the loss of nearly two days, it may be shorter still. I believe that the time available in the cave will be minimal now – and we must have time to search for the Cellini. Don't you see?"

He stared at her and at the slight movement of her sensuous lips. Giaconda smile, he thought.

"You mean those over-grown schoolboys, Leander and Brucey, are keeping an eye on us and are going to follow, when we round Red Bluff?" She was laughing at him again.

"That's what I believe. You may think it's silly, but if Leander sees you talking to me, we could have trouble. Not from Brucey – at least not until we reach the cave. But, I don't want any delays and argy-bargy on the beach, if the boy decides to create a scene. They won't know who you are in that get-up."

"Get-up! Thank you very much," she said in mock pique.

"Manon! You look smashing. I meant that your head scarf and your high-collared jacket will make it hard to identify you from a distance."

"They're both new. I hoped you would like them."

186

He could not help laughing. "You look super," he said. "But we've got a serious task in front of us. Are you sure you want to come?"

"Of course I do."

"Alright. Then give me a hand. I'll winch her on to the beach."

He fixed the cable and winched the dinghy down the smooth rock face. As it reached the sand, he detached the cable and then they hauled the dinghy into the sea, where Harry gave it a hearty shove. The boat immediately danced on the turbulent water.

"In you get!" he shouted. "And face the sea."

As Manon clambered aboard Harry pushed the boat out. Manon picked up the oars while Harry leaped into the bouncing dinghy. He quickly grasped the oars which she passed to him; and then he was pulling strongly out to sea and the waves were soaking them both with spray.

"Can you bail?" Harry yelled.

Manon nodded and started to bail out the sea water as it splashed in.

It was much harder to row than Harry remembered, but of course he had Manon's extra weight to pull. The unforeseen complication of meeting Manon worried him, but he decided that he really had no option with such a determined young woman. In any case if he had refused to take her, she could have made all sorts of difficulties to delay him.

When they were parallel with Red Bluff point and had begun to change course, the wind buffeted the dinghy as it rose and plunged on the rolling sea. Meanwhile Manon was leaning forward, head down and working continuously bailing out water. If he had any doubts about her presence he could see what an advantage it was to have her bailing so indefatigably. In fact he wondered if he could have reached this far without her help. As they moved under the lea of the

Bluff, they both felt the atmospheric menace of the sheer rock, towering over them.

"Can you see the cave?" Harry shouted.

Manon looked through the spray and shook her head. "No, no." But after she raised her hand to protect her eyes from the salt water, she nodded vigorously in contradiction of her words as she cried out, "Yes. Yes, I caught a glimpse of the opening."

Steadily the boat closed in under the vast maw of the Bluff. As on the previous occasion, Harry aimed the dinghy at the shiny, wet shelf of rock lying before the black entrance to the cave while he peered over his shoulder to check his position.

"Hold on!" he yelled as he steadied the dinghy for the last, swift pull on the oars.

A wave slapped the side of the boat, as it shot on to the rock apron, sending it spinning sideways so that Harry and Manon and the oars and satchel were all jettisoned in a heap. The boat itself then threatened to overturn on top of them, as it perched precariously on its side, juddering to the rhythm of the waves. In haste they scrambled up and pulled sharply at the boat.

"Lay it across the entrance. That way we'll hear if the boat is disturbed. It'll be our signal – if we are followed – that they've arrived." He threw the satchel ahead as they pushed the boat over the rocks.

Breathing heavily he said, "That's fine. Now we'll pull it across the opening, when we get inside the cave." At the same time he picked up the satchel and eased it over his shoulders.

"We must get a move on." He wrenched the torch out of the satchel. "Come on."

Light from outside dimly touched the interior of the cave, illuminating the wet rock. The torch beam picked out individual features: the spine of rock lying diagonally across the floor and the strange, theatrical platform and ramp at the back. The permanently wet conditions and the high, jagged ceiling above combined to create a sombre background in this secret place.

Harry hurried across the rocks and up the ramp to the centre of the platform with Manon close behind. In the middle he knelt down and peered along the torch's light into the crevice.

"Manon, would you hold the light while I see what I can find?"

Without a word she took the torch from him and directed the beam into the crevice beside him. Harry lowered himself on to his stomach, feeling with his right hand down the sides of the crevice, and leaning over so that his shoulder was supported against the rear wall.

"No inlet there," he reported. "Am I in the middle?"

"Try further on – the way you're facing."

He pushed himself along the rock and again paused to feel down inside the crevice for the hidden niche.

"No. But there's a long crack rising to the surface of the rock. I'll try it further on." He dragged himself awkwardly on again, and then leaned over once more.

Manon heard him exclaim, but could not catch his words above the dull roar of the sea. She saw his shoulders move and she lowered her arm to keep the torch light ahead of his searching fingers. Harry was lifting himself slowly and cautiously, pressing himself into a kneeling position.

"Is this it?" he asked as he stood upright.

They bent their heads together to examine a metal container illuminated by the torch. It was about the size of a biscuit box, quite plain, although if there had been any decorations on it, they would have been visible no longer under the ugly discolouration and encrustations. It was a curious and dramatic moment, if this was indeed the fabulous casket, to lift it from its resting place of centuries since the other Leander Penhalion had put it there. The box was oblong and heavy. Harry pushed it carefully into the satchel.

"Back towards the entrance, Manon," he said.

She led the way down the slope and over the floor of the cave, littered with loose rocks. Stepping over the rock spine, she reached the opening, where the dinghy lay obscuring most of the entrance.

Harry said, "Keep to your left. Behind those rocks before the boat. We shall be out of sight there and yet we'll have a commanding view."

They stumbled round the many boulders which, as Harry noted, formed a minor barrier at about waist height and provided what, as he recalled, the Infantry Manual had described as "cover from both view and fire". They lowered themselves behind the boulders; and he peeped over the top to see the general lay-out before him. Satisfied, he sank down, setting the satchel at his feet against a rock which was shaped like a stepping stone. Then, he withdrew the crowbar from the satchel, passing it to Manon with a faint smile.

"Look after yourself," he said.

He kept the satchel at his side and settled down to wait.

In the shed amidst the scrubland overlooking the sea, Parkinson and Leander were alarmed to see a girl walk along the shore to the rocks, where Guest was standing. Several times they handed each other the binoculars, back and forth, so as to examine her closely. This was an entirely unexpected development. It was important to know who the girl was, in view of the many uncertainties which lay ahead. But however long they scanned her head through the glasses, she never turned towards them, even when she climbed into the dinghy at the water's edge.

"Who the hell is it?" asked Parkinson. "Damn! She could spoil everything."

"It doesn't look like my sister. I've never seen her in that head scarf or jacket. But she won't look this way ever. I can't see her face."

As Guest rowed out to sea, the men talked over what could be done. It was Parkinson who made the decision.

"We might miss the chance. We can't risk that. Let's go, and we can always back-peddle if the girl turns out to be a potentially dangerous witness."

When Guest rowed the dinghy out of sight round the Bluff, Leander picked up the outboard motor and staggered outside with it. As soon as Leander's back was turned, Parkinson swiftly seized the opened brandy bottle and took a long swig from it before slinging the haversack over his shoulder and following him.

Previously Leander had hacked a rough passage through the scrub so that, although it meant they could exit to the beach, the path could hardly be identified as such from the shore. The wind and the rain, which was beginning to fall, beat into their faces as they hurried out to the boat. Leander looked round.

"All clear!" he called. "No one in sight."

"Just as well," commented Parkinson. "Let's get this thing down quick." He pitched the haversack into the bottom of the boat as Leander clipped on the engine.

They winched the boat on to the beach. Working together, they soon had the dinghy over the sands to the water, where Parkinson clambered into the boat as Leander pushed it out and jumped in after him. Both were soon soaked by the waves. While Parkinson rowed, Leander pulled repeatedly on the starter cord of the outboard motor which spluttered into life on the fourth tug. At a steady speed they set off in pursuit of Harry Guest and the unknown girl, as Parkinson drew in the oars.

It was a choppy run, but the boat soon rounded the point and headed for the centre of the Bluff. When they reached the entrance to the cave, they aimed the boat at the rock shelf. During the run-in, Leander cut the engine and snapped the unit out of the water, while Parkinson took over control of the boat as he pulled on the oars. The dinghy landed heavily and they climbed out, heaving it to safety at the back of the rocks.

Parkinson saw the outline of the second dinghy which had been laid across the cave mouth.

"Bloody hell!" he said. "They've put it there to act as a warning, so they'll know if anybody follows them."

"Of course," Leander replied. "Guest knew we'd follow. It doesn't matter. But I wonder what he's told that girl."

"We'll find out soon enough," said Parkinson as he brought out the crowbar and the torch from the haversack. "Here, you take the torch." He passed it to Leander.

They were ready and moved over to the boat lying by the cave. Parkinson gave it a hard push. The bottom of the boat dragged noisily over the surface of the rocks.

Inside the cave, there was not more than two minutes to wait before they heard the muffled thump of the landing boat and voices calling out. After a pause, the dinghy at the entrance wobbled until, with a rasping sound, it was forced back by some eighteen inches. Two men appeared making no effort to conceal their presence, but as they bent forwards to shuffle under the cave's arch and enter the gloom, it was not possible to recognise them immediately. When they straightened up and one of them switched on a torch, Parkinson and Leander were clear to see standing there. The lugubrious expression on Parkinson's face gave him the air of a melancholy beachcomber. Leander hung back, hesitant. Harry could see that both Parkinson's hands were full, but the light from the torch had not yet picked out what he was actually holding.

"Mr. Parkinson, isn't it?" Harry called.

Part 3: Return to Cornwall: September 1946

At once the two men instinctively crouched down and Leander swung his torch in the direction from which he had heard the voice.

As there was no reply, Harry asked, "What brings you here?"

"Who is that?" asked Parkinson angrily.

"It's Harry Guest," said Leander.

"Yes, it's me - Harry," he confirmed. "I hope you are not going to try any more of your rough stuff."

There was still no response. Harry continued. "Let me remind you. When I discovered this cave and managed to enter it, you followed me in. I did not know this at the time, but I found out later. It was only two days ago that I came. Got it now?"

He paused but neither man spoke.

"You thought that I could save you a lot of trouble by finding the Cellini, which we all believe is hidden in the cave. When I found the Cellini, you planned to take it from me. I believe that you came up behind me, as I was searching the crevice at the back of the raised platform of rock, and I think you made a silly mistake: you saw me beginning to rise to my feet and then you struck me down from behind. You thought I had found the Cellini – but I hadn't found it. I was just picking up my torch which I had switched off to conserve the battery. Is that correct?"

The men stayed silent.

"I say that you struck me down, but I did not know until later who it was or why. In fact I thought that I must have slipped and injured myself. When I came to, it was dark in the cave which was filled with water from the incoming tide by then. Can you imagine what it must have been like? It took me a while to pull myself together and I had a very sore head. You left me to drown, didn't you? Why?"

Parkinson could restrain himself no longer.

"It's not true!" he cried out.

"Well, let's see. I managed to swim down into the pool in the cave and out to the bay and back to the shore. Not bad against the currents and with a splitting headache. When I got to the place where the dinghies are berthed, what do you think I found? Surprise: the boat I rowed out to the cave had been returned to its berth. And how do you think the boat got back?"

"You've no proof!" shouted Parkinson, his voice echoing round the cave.

"Ah, but there's something else – something I found in the dinghy – the one named Jill – the one which I rowed out to the cave – I found a watch. It had an interesting and rather special engraving on the back plate. Let me see if I can remember it. It was 'to L. from G. 1935' with an inscription from a verse of Christopher Marlowe's. Poor Kit, who tried to protect his guilty secret, his treasure, his Cellini, through the efforts of his boyfriend, the first Leander Penhalion – fancy drawing the two Leanders together across the years! But, back to facts and the inscription on the watch: 'L' for Leander and 'G' for Geoffrey, wouldn't you say? – the nickname, Brucey, was to come later. And the fact that I found the watch in that particular dinghy could have one meaning only – that Leander rowed my dinghy back from the cave and without knowing it, his watch dropped onto the bottom of the boat under duckboards, when the strap broke. What do you say to that?"

Before either of the men could answer the questions, there was a scrabbling next to Harry as Manon stood up and leaned on the rocks. "Is this true, Leander?" Her voice was shaking with emotion.

When there was no reply, she called out, "You fool, Leander! How could you let yourself be drawn into attempted murder by that evil man?"

Her words, spoken with passion, sparked the astonished Leander to shout out, "No. It wasn't like that."

"What was it like then?" she cried.

194

Part 3: Return to Cornwall: September 1946

"He didn't mean to…" Leander began.

"Shut up!" shouted Parkinson. "And that's enough yap from all of you. You can prove nothing. It was an accident, and we tried to get Guest back, but we were overtaken by the tide."

The trembling light from Leander's torch highlighted the tense scene, and Harry saw that Parkinson was holding a crowbar in one hand and a pistol in the other hand. Harry said quietly to Manon, "Get down".

Leander, with the passing seconds, had time to overcome his surprise at hearing Manon's voice and also to absorb the impact of her wounding words. He called out, "It was an accident. And what are you doing here with Guest? What the hell's going on? We stayed the night together when I last saw you earlier in the week, and you said nothing about meeting Guest in the bay. How could you deceive me? What kind of friend are you? And what are you doing here? I'm the only one who has any right to the Cellini. You're interlopers."

As he finished speaking, Parkinson swung round and smashed the crowbar savagely against the young man's arm. Leander let out a shriek of pain and fell to the rocks, clasping his fractured limb.

Parkinson shouted, "You little rat! You told me you spent the night at your home. And all the time you were with that whore."

Harry intervened. "That's enough of that. Calm down, Mr. Parkinson. Let me remind you. We're all short of time. And we mustn't waste it, if we're to return to dry land in one piece."

Instead of cooling the situation Harry's words provoked Parkinson further, not least for reminding him of Harry's presence. Parkinson lifted his right hand, pointing his pistol in Harry's direction. His next words came out like a stunning irrelevance; and at once Harry understood the source of the man's burning hatred for him.

"You bastard! You called me a poofter. And nobody's going to say that and get away with it."

"Stop it! Stop behaving like a silly school boy. And put that pistol down this minute." It was Manon, the ex-WREN officer speaking with the voice of authority. She had remained standing in spite of Harry's warning to get down.

Parkinson appeared to respond to her order, and Harry watched as he lowered the pistol, but his hand was quivering with outraged emotion. Suddenly the cave was filled with a sharp explosion, the shock-waves of which reverberated about the rocks. It was accompanied by the sound of a high-pitched whine, the noise of a ricocheting bullet. It looked as if Parkinson, in his tense state, had squeezed the trigger of his pistol and fired it accidentally. He was trembling. The acrid smell of cordite carried in the moist atmosphere, stronger than the brine of the sea.

Harry had been standing beside Manon all this time. When the pistol fired, she had dropped abruptly, falling heavily. At first he thought that she had ducked instinctively, as the gun fired, and had slipped, but then in the half light he saw her white face. In the centre of her forehead there was a small, black hole with a minute trickle of blood oozing from it.

It took Harry several seconds to react.

"Oh no!" he said. "Oh no! Say it's not true. Oh my God!"

Leander rose painfully, grasping his damaged arm. He was terrified.

"What is it? What is it?"

Harry stared at the two men.

"She's dead!" he said.

He knelt beside Manon, his hand reaching for the pulse at her wrist, but he was sure that she was dead.

Leander stumbled up. He rounded the corner of the boulders and collapsed by Harry. Trembling with shock, he

196

began to sob hysterically, his uninjured arm about the dead girl's neck.

Parkinson stepped forwards, too, and stopped. Harry realised that there was acute danger in the situation while Parkinson remained armed. The man was like one drugged and the pistol was shaking in his hand.

Harry shouted at him, "Put it away. Look what you've done already. You've killed her."

Parkinson walked carelessly, as in a dream, over to the rock barrier and stared at Manon's body as it lay at an angle, eyes wide open. He glared at the dead girl, his right arm lowering until the pistol was pointing at the floor of the cave.

The moment had come for Harry to act. He steadied himself with both hands on top of the rock and placed one foot on to the stepping stone. Then he threw himself over the boulders in a flying tackle, landing with his shoulder hard against Parkinson's knees so that the man fell over with a cry of mingled pain and alarm. The pistol, however, was not dislodged by the fall and Harry tried to grab hold of it; but fear galvanised Parkinson who raised himself with the angry yell of "You bastard!" as he struck out at Harry. They grappled and, as they rolled over together, they wrestled painfully on the sharp rocks. Parkinson was able to free his right arm and to point his pistol at Harry. His hand was trembling when the pistol fired again. The roar and whine of the ensuing ricochet, as the bullet struck the rocks and howled off, were magnified in the confined space. He felt no pain and so he believed that Parkinson had missed him, but he might have no second chance to act. With the strength that sometimes comes in response to crisis, he lifted Parkinson bodily. There followed a desperate wrestling for control of the pistol as Parkinson tried to disengage himself from Harry's hold. Breaking free he struck out furiously, and in the mêlée both men crumpled together in a heap. There was a third explosion as the pistol was fired for the last time.

That was all. As the shock waves of the explosion faded, another and more menacing sound came to Harry's ears: the sea, the tide was on the turn. He stared at Parkinson as he cautiously released himself from his shrinking grip. Parkinson was still. Harry moved him over so that the thin light from outside fell directly on to his face. Parkinson had accidentally shot himself during the fight; there was a gaping wound on the side of his head. Harry felt the man's chest, but the heart was not beating. For a moment he continued staring in appalled disbelief until he heard a movement above him. He looked up into the eyes of Leander, standing distraught, somehow smaller, a totally lost look about him as he held his arm, obviously in great pain.

Harry said, "I'm sorry. He killed himself. It was an accident."

Leander's instant reply was, "You'll hang for this. I saw what happened. I'm going for the police." His face was distorted with grief and fear and shock, and tears streamed down his cheeks. He turned and quickly walked to where the boat lay across the entrance.

The sea was beginning to flow into the cave. Harry realised that he must move fast. Suddenly it was clear what he should do. The two bodies must be dragged above the water line, so that they would lie undisturbed by the turbulence of the incoming tide, which would otherwise dash the floating corpses against the rocks. He would put them on to the rear platform, where they could be retrieved, somehow, later. But first of all, there was Leander. He ought to see if he needed help.

As he hastily picked his way through the swirling water, he found that Leander, incredibly, had managed to launch the dinghy, although the sea was running high. However, he had not yet been able to try to start up the outboard motor. Single handed he was endeavouring to pull on one oar to clear the boat from the front rocks before the cave. As Harry watched, a wave scooped the dinghy, as if it were a toy, and lifted it high in the air. The little craft hung, suspended for what seemed like several seconds, before crashing upside down on the rock ledge with such force that the underside of the boat was swept violently back on the shelf, leaving one end bobbing in the sea with Leander trapped underneath. Harry jumped forwards and tried to release Leander by heaving at one end of the boat. Unfortunately his efforts had the effect of shifting the boat so that it swung upwards, assisted by the tide, and at the same time Leander's inert body was sucked away on a powerful current. Face down he floated round the edge of the rocks and beyond the shelf. The disintegrating boat was promptly washed after him by the next wave. It all occurred so quickly. There was nothing more that Harry could do; Leander was disappearing rapidly in the swell.

Some situations are so shocking that necessary subsequent actions follow automatically. As an automaton Harry set about doing what must be done. He picked up Manon's body in his strong arms and carried her to the platform, where he laid her down, brushed the wet hair from her face and left her hands crossed on her breast. Parkinson, he dragged and deposited just short of where he gauged that the water would rise, at the top of the ramp. As he leaned down to straighten the body, he noticed the strong smell of brandy on the lips.

Handling the two dead weights successively up the long ramp had been exhausting, but there could be no let up. It was time to go. The sea was tumbling into the cave and filling the interior. He returned once more to where Manon lay. Stopping at her side, he kissed her cheek and said, "Goodbye, Manon."

As he clambered back to the boulders, where he had waited with Manon a short while before, he wondered how he was going to get out, but he held on to the thought that he had only recently done it before and without a boat. At the worst he could swim to the shore. He picked up the satchel, buckled it up securely and slung it round his shoulders.

The next half hour was a nightmare. Looking back, after reaching the beach, he was surprised at how little recollection he had retained of the details of his struggle. He did launch the boat Jill after several failed attempts, when the dinghy was tossed back on the shelf. Luck and his determination, in equal measure, got him away. Then it was just a matter of rowing and rowing against the wind and the rain and the heavy swell.

XVII

Bill Tregoran was taking Patch for a walk. He was plodding along the foreshore and Patch was scampering happily as the wind blew sand in his face. They were approaching the curious sliver of land called St. Hilda's Rise which pushed out into the sea at a right angle to the beach. Sheets of water, driven by the gale, were periodically flung high as waves broke on the projecting rocks. As Bill came nearer to the finger of land, he saw something floating in the sea. He paused at the water's edge, where he noticed several pieces of broken timber bobbing on the back of the waves as they streamed across the deep green surface of the dark water; and on the sand too for about a hundred yards, he spotted smashed wood littering the shore. One long shaft lay ahead of him. He picked it up and examined it. There was no doubt about it, the wood was part of the shattered side of a dinghy. Painted on one edge was the name Jack.

He propped the drift wood over his shoulder and stared at the sea. As he gazed over the waves, his eyes settled on a larger and more solid shape. Just visible, half submerged, sometimes disappearing but constantly surfacing, the current was taking the object rapidly, swinging it in a steady, swirling dance, up and down, round and forwards.

201

He knew what it was. On this dangerous coast it was not the first, drowned corpse he had seen. The body, as far as he could make out in the twilight, was travelling, face down, towards the elbow nook of St. Hilda's Rise. He judged that if he aimed at the nook, he would be in a good position to pull the body ashore. Breaking into a run, he found his thoughts speeding ahead: who could it be? Somebody from the Red House? He remembered that the dinghy Jack was one of two owned by the Guest House.

When he reached the nook, he stopped to wait for the waves to bring the pathetic burden in. The body floated closer until he was able to step into the sea, seize the sodden clothing and assist the momentum of the waves to bring the corpse ashore. He dragged the body clear of the tide line, shouting at Patch to keep away. Then he looked down at the slim figure of a young man on his stomach, one broken arm lying at an awkward angle to the body. Taking a deep breath, he pulled the corpse onto its back. And there were the sightless eyes in the handsome face of Leander Penhalion.

Satisfied that the body was clear enough from the tide for the time being, Bill called Patch to him and set off towards the brow of the low ridge, which ran parallel with the shore, because he knew that Penwithin Manor was situated over there. Lady Trembath, who opened the door herself in response to his urgent ringing of the doorbell, was distressed to learn of his news and immediately invited him inside to make his telephone call. He spoke to the police. They would send a police car and ambulance to the nearest point to St. Hilda's Rise as soon as possible, and meet him on the beach. Meanwhile he was to safeguard the body.

Returning the separate ear-piece to the holder on the old-fashioned telephone stand, Bill looked up at Lady Trembath, white-haired, anxious, standing beside him.

"May I telephone the Red House, please? The worst part is next. I must inform the Penhalions."

202

She nodded without speaking and he lifted the receiver to wait for the operator to answer. It took several minutes, but at last the telephone was ringing in the hall at the Guest House. Alex answered.

"Can I speak to Mr. Penhalion, please? This is Bill Tregoran."

Alex told him her parents were out.

"I have very bad news for you, then, Alex. I've just 'phoned the police after finding Leander on the shore. He's been drowned."

In a brief exchange of words he confirmed that the police had arranged to meet him at St. Hilda's Rise to receive her brother's body.

Alex was standing in the hall of the Red House as Harry entered. He heard the grandfather clock striking the half hour at 7.30 p.m.; it was the emergency hour, when they had agreed that Alex was to go to the beach if he had not returned. She was speaking to somebody on the telephone, and he could see her anxious face peering at him.

Harry pointed upstairs and mouthed the words, "See you when you're free", but he realised from the look on her face that she already knew – perhaps no detail, but instinctively, she knew that something had gone terribly wrong. She stared at him as she watched him mount the stairs. He went into his bedroom, casting the satchel on his bed, and slowly returned to the door. He heard Alex replace the earpiece of the telephone with an emphatic click, and then her distressed cry from below: "Harry!"

He stepped through the door on to the landing in time to see Alex's red hair as she came into view, running up the stairs. When she turned her head, he could see her appalled expression. Now it was confirmed that she knew. Had the wreckage been discovered already? Surely poor Leander's body would have been swept out to sea by the currents?

At the top of the stairs Alex rested both hands for a moment on the round, decorated, mahogany ball which crowned the sturdy handrail at its junction with the guard on the landing. As she paused, he saw that her hands were trembling. Their eyes met and each understood the other's thoughts. She rushed to him with a cry and flung herself into his arms, shaking. Harry clutched her to him burying his face in her hair. She was sobbing violently.

Presently he whispered in her ear, "What do you know?"

Alex, holding his arm with both hands, leaned back to look into his eyes. "Leander is dead," she said. "Drowned."

"Who was that on the 'phone?"

"Your friend, Bill Tregoran. He's just found Leander at St Hilda's Rise with the remains of the dinghy Jack. And he's waiting there for the police."

Harry continued to stare at her with his red, tired eyes, which reflected his total, physical and emotional exhaustion. At last he said, "But you don't know..."

She interrupted, more in control. "Yes, I do. I did before the call. I felt it. I knew it was a disaster."

"Wait, wait. You don't know."

"Yes, I do."

"How can you?"

"Tell me, then."

Harry told her quite simply, briefly, of the deaths in the cave.

When he had finished, she said, "Yes, I did know before, but I also knew it when Bill told me that Leander had been found and the boat smashed and nobody else there. For a moment, before you came in, I thought that you..." Her voice trailed off.

"I couldn't bear another moment without knowing if you..."

Harry pulled her to him, pressing his face against her cheek. She began crying again with fierce sobs. When she was quieter, she said, very softly, "I love you."

Part 3: Return to Cornwall: September 1946

There was a pause before Harry spoke. Why did it have to be now, in the midst of catastrophe? Why now? But he knew and he knew that he had always known. He clasped her tightly, saying over and over again, "I love you."

They were interrupted by the sound of crunching gravel as a vehicle crossed the drive, but it was only a car reversing from the road in order to turn about. Harry pressed his arm round Alex's shoulders and guided her into his bedroom which they entered, leaving the door ajar so that Alex could step out to the landing if she heard the family return. Then, they were in each other's arms. For a while they clung together as if they would never break away from their first lovers' kiss. In the end it was Alex who parted them, gently placing her hands on his chest as she lowered herself on to the small, round, chintz covered chair. She wanted to know more.

Harry perched himself on the bed. It was time to tell her everything. He began to go over the whole business, including the details of how he had been attacked and abandoned in the cave in the first visit and how they had passed the car with Parkinson and Leander in Lavington afterwards. When he stopped, they gazed into each other's eyes. Nothing could shock her anymore. As she did not speak, Harry added, "They were all tragic accidents. And now, I must go. I must go to the police and report what has happened."

He saw from the expression on her face that she was transformed, strong and once more self possessed. She said abruptly, "Why?"

Intuitively he understood what she meant by the question, but what should he do? She meant: why go through the torment of a full scale police enquiry? He was the sole surviving witness of the events, and there was no telling where his report could lead. What of a murder charge even? or a charge of manslaughter? And, too, what about all the publicity and the pressures on the family and on Maurice Lescaut? Surely it was bad enough already?

Alex said, "The police will assume – won't they? - that Leander and Manon both drowned in the wrecked dinghy. The fact that Manon's body has not appeared would be natural enough. The currents do funny things. She could have been swept out to sea, couldn't she? You see what I mean, don't you?"

Harry did not want to discuss it yet, but he nodded his head non-comittally. "Yes, Manon would be reported missing," he said.

She went on, "And as for Parkinson, we don't know where he stayed, but there's no reason anyway to connect his visit with the other two. It's more than likely that Parkinson's visit would go unnoticed. Obviously he would not want people to know what he was up to, and so he would have kept under cover somewhere. Wouldn't he?"

Harry did not reply. It was too difficult to face.

"Don't you agree?" Alex asked.

"Yes," he said unconvincingly.

"The cave has kept its secret for more than three hundred years. Why shouldn't it now become a tomb for the next three hundred years?"

Harry stared at her, astonished at the audacity of what she was saying.

"You don't really mean we should do nothing more?" he asked. "Do you?"

"Yes, I do. I see it with absolute clarity. There's no point. No need for anybody else to be hurt unnecessarily. Nothing to do – can you truly imagine what it would be like for my parents – leaving us out of the considerations – if we had swarms of police and newspaper reporters round the house for days and days and days? The risk is minimal. And even if the bodies were found one day what proof can there possibly be that you were in any way connected?"

When she had finished speaking, Harry kissed her.

Part 3: Return to Cornwall: September 1946

After a while she leaned back and looked into his eyes and said, "Tell me, Harry, how are you after all you've been through? With that quite incredible row back from the cave, let alone everything else? Are you hurt – as well as exhausted as I can see – and your head too?"

"I'm just very tired."

Alex spoke softly, "I can see you're still worried, but you're worn out. You need a good night's sleep. It wouldn't be too late to wait till the morning before you decide. The delay could be because you have suffered from shock." But she believed that he had already decided to remain silent. She thought he would not go to the police.

Alex said that she must telephone Vivian with the news, as he was away. Before she left the room, they embraced again until, reluctantly, she turned away and descended the stairs to the hall. Left to himself, Harry was changing out of his damp and soiled clothes, when he noticed that his tracksuit was stained with blood from Parkinson's mortal wound. He thought that Alex had not spotted it, because the stain merged with the dark material. The bedroom mirror showed him that the sea had washed his face clean during the row back from the cave. As he examined the tracksuit top, he caught sight of a slight snag on one side. Picking up his shirt, he saw that there was a slit in the cotton at a point which corresponded with the tear on the tracksuit. When he looked at his body in the mirror, turning sideways, he saw a long thin bruise and scuffing of the skin between his hip bone and his ribs. The graze must have been caused by the second bullet which Parkinson had fired, the one which he had aimed at Harry. He breathed in deeply and bent his shoulders to each side, but he could feel no pain; and he thought how fortunate he was not to be lying on the cold rocks under Red Bluff.

His thoughts were disturbed by the noise of the Penhalion's car entering the drive, and he hurried down to be with Alex. When she broke the news to her parents, Jean

207

cried and Dan looked grim. After many unhappy hours, the dreadful day drew to a close and they all retired to bed.

During the night Harry wakened from a nightmare. He dreamed that he was carrying the dead Manon in his arms. The encroaching sea in the cave was resounding in his ears. As he moved, he became aware of a feeling of compulsion to look down at his burden. Although he tried to avoid seeing Manon's face, he found himself staring at her wide open eyes. Her head was dangling, like a rag doll's, swinging as he walked and dripping blood which soaked into his tracksuit. When he stopped, he could see again her lovely face, disfigured by the tiny wound, but he saw also that the back of her skull had been blown away, revealing a seeping mess of grey and crimson brain. When he awoke, it took him some time to detach himself from the dream as he sat bolt upright in bed, trembling as if he was suffering from the effects of malaria, and his pyjama jacket was soaked with perspiration.

Gradually he calmed down, and as he became calmer, he remembered vividly the scene in the cave. The memory raised a parallel recollection in his mind. He found himself reciting in his head a verse from a poem by Rudyard Kipling which he had learned years ago. The poem told the story of the murder of a young British officer in the Far East:

> *"A Snider squibbed in the jungle –*
> *Somebody laughed and fled,*
> *And the men of the First Shikaris*
> *Picked up their Subaltern dead,*
> *With a big blue mark in his forehead*
> *And the back blown out of his head."*

That was where the nightmare was at least partly born. But, he thought, Manon had been unscathed except for the little black hole in her forehead. He wondered about it. Of course, it had been an accident, not a direct shot, and the

208

bullet – when the pistol was fired – shrieked in the echoing cave as it ricocheted off the rock, its power reduced as it penetrated the skull. The bullet must have lodged inside the head. That was the reason why there had been no horrific wound at the back of the head, where the bullet could have exited, and of course the pistol was less powerful than the Snider, the Indian rifle.

He got up quickly, drying off the sweat with his bathing towel and then dressed. He walked quietly out of the house, down the slope and up to Red Bluff point below which Manon lay. For a long time he sat with the wind blustering about his head in the early morning. Time passed and he had to stretch stiff limbs. He must have been there for an hour, because he became conscious of a brightening light which spread over the eastern sky. The dawn was coming. As the sky lightened, the birds began to sing.

XVIII

Leander's death cast a shadow over the Penhalion family. Meanwhile there was a succession of calls at the Red House from sympathisers and also from officials on duty, as news of the tragic drowning spread. Yet despite everything Harry and Alex found time early on to slip away on their own, because they were desperate to know what the casket contained. To date all their efforts to lift the lid had failed. Their endeavours, of course, were made more difficult because of the need to work without any possible interruption, whenever they could find an empty room for the purpose.

One morning they took the casket, covered by an old shawl, up to the attic. However after another fruitless attempt there, Alex said, "At this rate we're going to have to keep it hidden for some time. It can't stay any longer in your bedroom cupboard, and I want to show you a better place for it."

"Where is that?"

"Just above your head." She pointed to the roof, where a junction of rafters formed a hidden niche.

"Try it," she said. "I don't think it can be seen from below. The idea came to me years ago when I was trying to write a story about concealing treasure!"

210

"Really? And now you've got a real treasure to hide," he replied as he lifted the casket and pushed it into the niche. Then, with care, he began testing whether the object could be seen by the tallest possible person from any point in the attic. He stood on a stool, peering up at the rafters and kept repeating similar checks from further away until he was satisfied that it was invisible from anywhere up there.

Alex asked, "Will it do?"

"Yes, fine."

"In that case we can use it until we reach a firm decision about the casket's future. But, now, let's take it outside and have a go at opening it in a quiet place."

She was determined to have a really undisturbed attempt, away from the house on their own. Even in the attic they had to be alert for passers-by on the landing below.

When they descended from the attic, Harry brought the casket down still concealed in the shawl, as Alex turned off to the kitchen and spoke to Jean from the open door.

"Mummy, would you mind if Harry and I drove off for the day? We want to go beyond Western Cove and walk on the remote beach there."

"Of course not, dear," Jean replied. "You could both do with a blow of fresh air. We'll see you this evening."

In the autumn sunshine they drove out on the coast road beyond Lavington to an isolated strand which Alex knew. There they unfolded the car rug on long grass and sat together with their feet on the sand, holding hands beside the restless sea. The casket lay between them; its grimy scaly exterior seemed to hold unpropitious notice of its contents.

Because of the need for secrecy, it was not possible to obtain skilled assistance for opening the casket, which could otherwise be damaged in their inexperienced hands. So, they set to using a small screwdriver covered at the tip by a strip of strong Hessian to protect the surface of the casket. Taking it in turns they pressed the tool with the greatest care against the slim edges from different angles. After half an hour there was no movement. They seemed to be making no progress until Harry thought he detected a slight shift on one side, and shortly after, to their astonishment, the lid slipped open easily.

They stared inside.

Fitting perfectly into its specially prepared mould lay a gold and silver figure. Harry placed his hand across the container's mouth and, with Alex's help, turned it upside down. Immediately the contents dropped into his open palm, so that he could clasp it and set it upright on the blanket.

It was a crucifix. Christ himself was made of gold and hung from a silver cross, which was secured to a solid, square ebony base. On each of the four sides of the base were pure gold miniature panels with raised images illustrating aspects of the life of Jesus; and each corner of the base was supported by the strong body of a silver fish, long and curved so as to hold the cross upright. Perhaps because of the meticulous design, the hermetic sealing of the lid of the casket had proved so effective that the crucifix was well preserved. Indeed, it only needed polishing to make the surface shine. Alex rubbed the masterpiece with a duster from the car. Then, as they gazed at it, each experienced a feeling of peace.

Harry remembered the words which Benvenuto Cellini had written in his autobiography about that other, life-size crucifix which he had sculpted: "...one of the most difficult things in the world. It is a Christ of whitest marble on a cross of blackest marble..." In the gold and silver crucifix on its black pedestal, Cellini had again used the contrast of extremes to create an astonishing work of art.

Alex spoke several minutes later. "It's beautiful!" she said. "Oh, it's so beautiful."

The September sun was warm and a breeze off the sea kept them cool as they remained side by side looking at the

212

crucifix. As time passed they continued contemplating the unique magic of their discovery.

"What are you thinking?" Alex asked.

"I can only think of the word you used. It is so very beautiful."

Alex indicated the base of the crucifix.

"And do you see how he has taken the early Christian fish symbol to support it?"

"Yes. But, tell me about the fish."

"We had an enthusiastic young teacher at School who told us how the fish came from an acronym. The early Christians apparently took the letters from each of the words which proclaimed "Jesus Christ, Son of God, Saviour." The result – from the Greek original, that is – was Ichthus, the fish. Which became a widely adopted Christian symbol. It appeared later on rings and seals and, of course, on tombs, focusing their belief."

"What a fascinating idea!"

Stiff from squatting for so long, Alex slowly lay back, and shortly Harry joined her lying on the rug, where they stretched out together. Presently Harry's arm moved round her shoulder. He leaned over and kissed her, saying, "I love you."

An hour passed as they lingered beside the incredible Cellini figure which, unseen by them, had fallen sideways, disturbed by their soft movements until they lay quite still, blissfully happy in each other's arms.

At last Harry sat up. Then he began to talk enthusiastically. "Everything – and especially the Cellini – all go back to Kit Marlowe. And there's such a lot connected with Kit's life which is unexplained today. Mysterious. I read, for example, that it was necessary for Kit during his time at Cambridge to petition to receive his M.A degree, despite the fact he was entitled to it. And yet he was refused! Some thought that his many absences from the University was the cause. But it was more likely to be about ugly rumours."

"And all this was from your search at Plymouth library?" Alex asked.

Harry nodded. "The next thing for Kit was an astonishing turn-about. Only a few months later. By July in 1587 the University reversed the decision, and Kit got his M.A."

"What happened? Why the sudden change?"

"The answer is very odd indeed. I meant to tell you at the time, but we were too busy. I actually took a copy of the amazing letter about it. It's in my wallet."

"And?'

"It was a directive to the University from the Privy Council at the session where all the top people attended – and all signed the letter too."

Harry pulled out his wallet, took out a folded sheet of paper and passed it to Alex.

The letter read as follows: *Whereas it was reported that Christopher Morley was determined to have gone beyond the sea to Reames and there to remain, their Lordships thought good to certify that he had no such intent, but that in all his accions he had behaved himselfe orderlie and discreetelie wherbe he had done her majestie good service, and deserved to be rewarded for his faithful dealinge: Their Lordship's request was that the rumour thereof should be allaied by all possible means, and that he should be furthered in the degree he was to take this next commencement: Because it was not her majestie's pleasure that anie one emploid as he had been in matter touching the benefit of his Countrie should be defamed.*

Harry went on, "It was especially surprising support from the highest in the realm for the young twenty three year old Kit Marlowe. It also managed to say as little as possible in a masterly way."

He picked up the crucifix, turning it in his hand as he examined the various scenes created by the artist on each of the plinth's four panels. Meanwhile Alex was reading the copy letter and his notes.

"I still don't see what it was all about."

"I know. It's a puzzle. Maybe the document was trying to address a wider audience – to scotch a flood of rumours about Kit. It was being said, for instance, that Kit had Catholic leanings and, even, that he was a spy. And, above all, that he was a plotter – against the Queen – and that he had visited the English Catholic Seminary at Rheims."

"How does Rheims come into it?"

"Well, some historians think Kit was a member of Sir Francis Walsingham's Secret Service. If so, he would probably have gone there – to Rheims – to keep a sharp eye out for plotters: English Catholics being trained for the Priesthood could, it was thought at the same time be plotting, undercover, to overthrow the Queen, even to organise her assassination."

Harry leaned over and picked up the Crucifix again, peering at it before returning it to its mould. The lid of the casket closed easily now.

He said, "It's a real puzzle. Why on earth would Marlowe – in the first place – want to possess a crucifix? and why would he want to own it so badly that, apparently he was ready to risk his life to get his hands on it?"

Slapping sand from his legs, he added. "It's even more extraordinary – according to the Leander letter – he had only recently escaped the forgery charge. And that was just over six months before. Do you remember?"

They exchanged a questioning glance as Alex nodded.

Harry said, "I wonder, is it possible that while he was at Rheims, he was actually so persuaded by his religious instructors that he became a convert to the Roman Catholic faith? Whilst at the same time keeping quiet about it?"

She laughed. "What? A double agent? In the employ of Elizabeth's secret service and also attached to the Vatican's equivalent?"

"Oh – anything's possible in those turbulent, dangerous times." He smiled. "Anyhow, how else can we explain it? I see Kit Marlowe at the centre of a spider's web of intrigue. In the twilight world of Queen Elizabeth's secret service, he would have had to be very circumspect, especially when the Queen had virtually intervened for him in the matter of his M.A. – perhaps to qualify him for his secretive mission to Rheims. If his change of faith had ever been discovered, he would, in his special position, have been on the executioner's block in no time – a powerful incentive for keeping his conversion secret."

Alex shook her head and said, "What a tangled web."

"Even more tangled. There was a really nasty public informer called Richard Baines who drew up a list of allegations against Marlowe and presented it to the Privy Council - this was at the end of Kit's life. Sir Francis Walsingham had died some three years earlier, and Thomas Walsingham, the son of a cousin of his, was the intimate friend and patron of Kit. Incidentally only about four years after Kit's death, Queen Elizabeth, on a visit to Scadbury, knighted Thomas there. It adds another surprising dimension to Kit's standing amongst top people of his day."

Alex said, "It's all so interesting. What a trawl you've made of the library. But you were just going to tell me more about the dreadful Baines."

"Sorry. Yes, Baines's allegations show the other side of the coin. For example he said that Marlowe 'persuades men to Atheism' and also that 'all men in Christianity ought to endeavour that the mouth of so dangerous a member be stopped', meaning Kit, of course."

Alex cast her eyes up and said, "I'm lost. So much speculation and so many pieces of information. But at least one thing is clear – if I remember the Leander letter correctly – and that is the reason why the casket was provided for the crucifix. The letter says it was designed by Cellini himself to protect the precious thing during its owner's travels. Roads were very un-made up and bumpy in those days. And the owner, who was likely to be a Catholic, could take the crucifix with him, knowing that it would be undamaged, for his devotion while travelling."

"That's it. Nice and logical too."

It had begun to cool down, and so they returned to the car. Harry leaned forward and turned the ignition key. As the engine started, Alex asked about the future.

"What are we going to do with the crucifix? After all the centuries in the darkness it must come into the light for as many people as possible to see. In a museum surely?"

"Agreed, Alex, but we would still have more hurdles to take, more problems. Unfortunately as soon as you put the Cellini in the public eye enormous publicity is bound to follow, together with endless, probing questions: Where did you get it? Why has it only just come into public view? How can you claim that you own it? And so on."

Gloomily Alex said, "I see what you mean. The family would be brought into it, and we mustn't let that happen. And I can't bear the idea of facing all those clever, prying questioners gradually drawing out more and more details until they come upon the cave, and..." her words faltered.

"Oh, Alex, I'm sorry. But at the moment it does look as if we are trapped. We're too close to the problem, and too wrapped up in Leander's death, to think straight. Whereas it must, at least in the beginning have seemed quite different from Brucey's point of view."

"Why do you say that?"

"Brucey was obviously the kind of crooked specialist dealer who would have been in touch with other like dealers on the international scene. He would have known all the slippery ropes: where to seek a buyer, and just as important, he would have known how to overcome all the problems involved in avoiding customs, and so on, if – as I think would have been likely – he had searched overseas."

"He wouldn't still be able to get the full market price, though, would he?"

"No, Alex. But he'd certainly get a huge sum on the sale, justifying any risks he might take in the process, once he found the right buyer. It would have to be one of those rather absurd maniacs, wealthy enough to dwell on the unique and curious pleasure of owning and enjoying any highly valued or famous example of supreme art which only he can see."

Alex sounded sad as she said, "I'm afraid we're back where we started. The question remains, what are we going to do with the crucifix?"

Harry raised his hands for a moment from the steering wheel as if to clear the air. "We shall have to go on thinking and talking. There's nothing at present to do apart from that."

"So, we put the casket in the attic?"

"Yes, and it will be safe in the place you've chosen – for the time being of course."

But their worthy objective of exhibiting the crucifix where it would be kept in absolute safety and seen by the maximum number of men and women possible was a long way from being achieved. Their guilty secret still blocked the way.

XIX

St. Hilda's was a typical, small Cornish church, situated on a hilltop two miles outside Lavington to the North-west. It was squat and solid, built of granite and having a grey, tiled roof and neat tower, surmounted by four disproportionately tall, slim pinnacles on each corner and a white flagstaff in the centre at the top. On this late, October morning a shaft of sunlight pierced the low cloud, illuminating the tower and the graveyard and the surrounding, granite, boundary wall. Far off the hills rolled green down to the sea which was visible as a deep blue line on the horizon.

Harry approached the church up the steep path, holding a large spray of red roses upright in one hand so that the flowers, in their wrapping, leaned against his shoulder. As he reached the lych-gate, a single sonorous bell began to toll. At the same time a number of pigeons, disturbed by the ringing bell, rose flapping their wings noisily as they flew off together in an irregular 'S' shape across the cloudy sky.

In the far corner of the churchyard, on the side nearest to the sea, was an open grave. It was the morning of Leander Penhalion's funeral. There had been a 'bus strike at St. Aubyn and the flowers, ordered by the family for the service, could not be supplied in time, according to a telephone message received at breakfast in the Red House. Harry had volunteered to drive in to collect the flowers and had arranged to meet Alex and the others at the Church. In fact he had been quicker than expected, and now he settled to wait for the family, sitting on the wooden bench outside the church. Then the bell stopped ringing and did not recommence until the first of the mourners started to arrive.

Harry let his mind go back over the events of the past, stressful weeks leading to the inquest. The Coroner's verdict was death by drowning – misadventure. Late on the night that Leander's body had been found, Maurice Lescaut had telephoned. Fortunately for the family Harry had taken the call and he told Maurice of Leander's death. Maurice had sounded upset. He had telephoned to enquire whether Manon was at the Red House, explaining that neighbours had reported seeing Leander and Manon together on the previous day. Now he feared that Manon may have been with Leander in the wrecked boat which Harry told him about.

It was the first time Harry had come face to face with the dissembling consequences of his decision to withhold from the police the facts of the deaths of Manon and Parkinson. As the days passed and Manon failed to return, the local belief grew that she had drowned with Leander, and that her body must have passed the catchment at St. Hilda's Rise and been swept out to sea on the currents.

And what about George Parkinson? He would surely become anxious at some stage as weeks and months passed with no news of his brother, Brucey. Obviously he would eventually contact the Metropolitan police, maybe reporting him as a "missing person". Little was known about George except for his reputation as a hard-headed businessman. The two brothers' contacts through their joint business affairs were infrequent, because of their entirely separate responsibilities for Antiques and for Books respectively, and their personal lives were likely to have been quite apart from each other.

Harry felt that it was getting cold, so he wandered into the porch of the church, where there were two benches fixed to the walls facing each other. He sat on the right-hand side. As he did so, his eyes followed the line of the churchyard wall and beyond to the green expanse of wild land falling away to the distant sea. Far off was a glimpse of Red Bluff point. Staring there, his imagination conceived a terrible vision of the solitary pair, who in life had detested one another and who in death lay together in the cave below the promontory on the unhallowed and remote rock platform. His troubled conscience, seeking consolation, brought to mind the last words in *Wuthering Heights*, where Catherine, standing in the moonlight near the graves by the moor, wonders "how any one could ever imagine unquiet slumbers for the sleepers in that quiet earth." He closed his eyes.

St. Hilda's church bell brought him back to the present as it began to toll its melancholy notes. The first of the mourners' cars pulled up into the space by the lych-gate. Fifty minutes later it was all over, both the service and the burial, and the cars were driving away.

Part 4:

Cornwall: September 1947

I

The stirring and uninhibited Victory celebrations were now only a blurred memory. As for the events in the cave beneath Red Bluff, they took place one year ago. Since then Harry and Alex had become engaged to be married.

Meanwhile Harry was enjoying a fresh holiday at the Red House before going to university in October.

At the end of the Summer on a bright September morning he was sitting in a corner of the Serpentine Food Bar in Plymouth. In front of him on the counter was a cup of coffee. Between sips of his drink he was reading an article in the daily paper, which was commenting on the progress being made with constitutional changes taking place in Northern Rhodesia. His concentration was interrupted by a shuffling movement further down the bar. Glancing up at the reflection in a long mirror at the back of the counter, he noticed a tall man wearing a chequered sports jacket, who was leaning forward to read the menu as he settled himself onto a bar stool. Something about the newcomer seemed familiar. As he watched, the man slowly raised his head so that Harry could see the outline of his face in profile. It was Brucey Parkinson. Harry's hand dropped against the saucer of his coffee cup causing a sharp clatter on the Formica top.

But, Brucey was dead. At the sound of clinking china the man turned slightly in his direction so that Harry could see his face from the front. No, it wasn't Brucey after all, but the man was very like him, only taller, older.

The episode shocked Harry, who stumbled as he pushed back the bar stool with a noisy gesture so as to give himself room to get out as quickly as possible. But, leaving the stranger behind did not remove the image of his face from Harry's memory, and the recollection haunted him for days, although he was determined not to worry Alex by telling her what had happened.

About a week later, Harry was standing in the long hall at the Red House when the telephone rang. In fact he was about to go outside as he heard Vivian answer the 'phone. Vivian called out, "It's for you, Harry."

"Really? I'm not expecting anybody." He stepped back into the house and down the hall, taking the 'phone from Vivian's hand.

"Hello. Harry Guest here."

"Good morning, Mr. Guest. You don't know me." The man's voice was deep and his vowels as he spoke were rounded, theatrical. "My name's Marlowe and I am a partner in a firm of solicitors, Gladwyn, Jessop and Williams of Penarth. My firm has been having difficulty tracing the whereabouts of a Trust beneficiary. Enquiries have established that Mr. and Mrs. Daniel Penhalion of the Red House by Red Bluff were at one time connected with the gentleman in question, namely Mr. Harry Guest."

"Yes. I've said that I'm Harry Guest."

"And may I ask if you have been associated for long with Mr. and Mrs. Penhalion?"

"We met for the first time, when I came here in 1938, before the war."

"You must be the gentleman I am seeking. May I ask if you stayed with them at this time last year, please?"

"Yes. I am a very close friend of the family."

226

"Thank you. Now, my firm wishes to write to you officially. Would it be in order, please, to address my communication to you direct at your present address? I mean, if it's not impertinent to ask, how long do you expect to be staying – or would you prefer me to post to your home address?"

"I'm here for another three weeks. But, what's this all about?"

"It is all quite straight forward. You are the beneficiary under a certain trust and there are facets of this latter trust which I am obliged to treat in confidence,"

"That's very interesting. I shall look forward to hearing from you, Mr. Marlowe."

"Good morning, then, Mr. Guest."

When Harry met Alex next, he told her had had received an unexpected call. "Somebody wanting to have this address to forward a letter. I hope it was O.K. to give the Red House until the end of the month."

"Of course, Harry, it is home to you."

On his own, however, Harry was puzzled by the 'phone call.

Don't know anybody – who would want to benefit me – wonder what it's all about – wait and see – won't say anything – don't want Alex to worry – but it's curious – so secretive and only a legacy – and what "facets" could there be? – I'll tell the family if it's good news – but hang on for a bit.

Some days later, when Harry had almost forgotten about the Marlowe enquiry, he received a large envelope, marked "Private and Confidential", with a Plymouth post mark on it. It was at breakfast and Harry picked it up from other envelopes waiting at the large Victorian side-board against the wall. Opening it he pulled out another, smaller envelope, also sealed, together with a single, separate sheet letter.

He read the brief note: "Attached to my letter is a sealed envelope which is for your confidential information as I have marked on it. I mention this, because you may then decide to open the second letter in private."

An anxious frown creased Harry's face as he folded the letter and slipped it with the envelope quickly into the inside pocket of his sports jacket. Nobody was in the dining room, so he went upstairs to his bedroom and sat down on the comfy bedside chair. Tearing open the second envelope he began to read the lengthy letter, which was written in a bold hand with ostentatious flourishes of the pen. He read the contents with growing alarm.

"I am writing to you about a man, well known to you, who disappeared during this month last year, in 1946. Ah, I think I must have your attention. Yes, I mean Brucey Parkinson.

"But, I must apologise straight away for my recent deception when I 'phoned concerning a Trust beneficiary – not true, I'm afraid, but I could not find a quicker method of getting your address. And I wanted to be able to keep things just between ourselves as I'm sure you will agree by the time you have read my letter to the finish.

"Let's return to Brucey. I wonder if you knew how fond of Christopher Marlowe's poetry he was. If Brucey was alive today he might well have expressed himself with lines from one of Marlowe's plays. But, first of all, let's be direct about Brucey's fate. You know – and I believe – that Brucey is dead, and that you murdered him.

"So our first quotation is from 'Tamburlaine the Great':

'I know, what it is to kill a man;
It works remorse of conscience in men,
I take no pleasure to be murderous.'

"Does that characterise your conscience?

"Never mind – let's move now towards my purpose with a sensible warning, so that there are no misunderstandings between us as to the danger which is near to both you and yours.

"My next line is also from the same play:

'Our life is frail, and we may die to-day.'

"Even as you read, your loved one is being closely observed. Just keep that thought to the forefront of your mind. And do not be so foolish as to endanger your Alex. Yes, I have heard about your fiancée – but you kept quiet about her on the 'phone, didn't you? A bit of 'second sight'? Never mind. But, remember, if you make one false move, then Marlowe's *'we may die to-day'* could become a certainty. Think about it.

"Which brings me to the real business of my letter. You will have gathered that I know what I am talking about, but have you guessed my source of information? Perhaps you have: the diary. But you overlooked the possibility that Brucey might leave behind him evidence enough to hang you, didn't you? Yet he did leave diaries. He kept several, but I only stumbled on them by accident recently. They were carefully hidden away. The last one is what matters, covering the year 1946, and it reveals most of the story – and what is not shown can easily be surmised. Let me explain what I mean and fill you in, so that you understand what cards I hold.

"To start with you made the extraordinary discovery of Kit Marlowe's Cellini in the secret cave beneath Red Bluff. And then you guided Brucey to its resting place. In the process you overcame the "Guardian Tides", as Kit Marlowe's boyfriend called them in the historic letter which you must have found, and which you cleverly copied out – and which I now hold! But, no marks for security on your part. Am I right? And there was somebody else involved, Brucey's friend, Leander. What happened to them both? Leander's death was easy, I think. You made it appear as if he died from drowning, as the coroner's verdict confirmed, but Brucey's body has never been discovered, because, as I guess, it lies where you callously left it, inside the cave. You thought you were safe, because the cave's existence is known to nobody else.

"But to business, you can see what I am leading up to? Yes, I want the Cellini. It has never appeared on the markets. What a sensation that would be! So, I want it. I shall therefore be in touch with you, when you have had time to absorb what I am telling you – and prepare yourself, so that our plans can be dove-tailed together for a smooth passage. Well, I am going to give you one more call at the Red House. And I give you advance warning – when I call you again, you will carry out my instructions immediately, without any delay and without question. Is that understood?

"Finally, attend to me, this is vital. You must speak to nobody, not to Alex and in no circumstances to the police.

"That's all for the moment. Await my call, and, above all remember your girl, Alex, and keep silence for her sake as well as for yourself.

Marlowe."

As he read the letter Harry felt his heart pounding. When he reached the end, he read the letter through a second time, slowly.

The shock of reading the blackmail letter brought with it a disabling fear, but this was soon replaced by hard thinking. His first reaction to the threat of violence was a decision to go to the police. In fact he picked up the 'phone and was about to dial the police when he changed his mind, returning the instrument to its cradle.

He closed his eyes, letting his thoughts drift across his mind. Let's see: the beginning – who is Marlowe? – of course I know. Only one person possible and I saw him recently. In the café mirror of the Serpentine Food Bar: Brucey's brother George. How can I unravel the turmoil I'm in? What about father's old friend, Jack Islington? He's a Q.C. What might he say on learning the facts? Jack's advice would be forthright.

"You seem to have decided against going to the police, Harry. Which is exactly what you should have done a year ago – at once. You were at that time influenced by the vivid picture of your situation, then, painted in your own mind and fuelled by Alex's impassioned pleas. This time around, as it were, your problems are more than doubled. Let's re-paint the picture from this moment.

"For a start Alex would be the key figure when the facts are published. Alex, more than you, would be the central object of criticism and ridicule. It could be said that she had withheld information from her parents, when she heard of your discovery of the Leander letter. It is also likely that she would be regarded as the person who authorised the search which you undertook for the Cellini – whatever you might try to represent – and therefore she would also be perceived to be responsible for acting as the spark which set off all the subsequent events. There would be ruthless cross-examination and sustained nation-wide publicity.

"As for the consequences of confession – if you took that line, imagine for yourself: a dreadful effect on the whole Penhalion family, already suffering from the loss of their younger son as a result of the series of events. And also your own family, don't forget. Think what it would mean. Far worse, really, than if the facts had been made known in 1946. After all, you stand condemned of deceit, moral cowardice and failing to protect the interests of a young woman – by your own words.

231

"Now, as for Parkinson. Once his identity has been established, the clearer everything becomes. George, you told me, is well known in the up-market circle of leading London antiques' dealers. He would therefore have vital contacts, as well as the specialist expertise at hand, necessary when it came to disposal of such a rare piece as the Cellini. In the light of the latter's recent history – whose details could hardly be disclosed – he is likely to aim to accept a lesser price than its open market value, by offering the masterpiece to a wealthy collector. Certainly someone known to be prepared to deal out of sight of the public, via some decidedly underground agency. Somebody prepared to pay less but still an outrageous figure for his personal pleasure – so that he, or a trusted few alone, would ever enjoy the sight of the Cellini again.

"I do not advise anything. You've got to pick up the pieces. But, the ghastly alternative – handling the blackmailer on your own – looks to me like being your better choice, so long as you assiduously recognise the grave and inherent dangers involved in attempting to deal with Parkinson by yourself. Mind you, that would never be the advice I would offer, if you had come to me in practice.

"Yet, notice the contrast. Alex should stay safe – subject to the way you set about the problem – so long as you keep in touch with Parkinson. A blackmailer loses his advantage when he carries out his threat against his victim! But, he could become very dangerous if, for example, a point should arise where he sees his own plan failing. As to yourself, look at your military training and your fitness, there's much on your side. Still, remember the powerful disadvantages: Parkinson believes he holds all the trumps in the game; he has absolute commitment; and the courage – or madness – to take the first step in the blackmailer stakes. Be careful."

Harry read through the Marlowe letter a third time. A curious yet obvious omission stood out. There was no mention of Manon. Her presence in the cave and her death could not of course have been recorded in the diary since Brucey died shortly after her death. All of which suggested that George Parkinson's sources of information were restricted to diary events.

Harry was angry at the deception used to contact him; the writer's facetious words, too, he found insufferable; and the absurd accusation that he had murdered Brucey infuriated him, not the least because he knew he had fallen into a trap of his own making. He would not be in this situation if in 1946 he had reported the cave deaths to the police.

A cold fury was blowing the cobwebs out of his mind, so that he felt his strength returning, bringing with it a confidence which the circumstances hardly warranted.

When Marlowe's call came through, it proved to be a complete anti-climax. Harry had been worrying about it, fearing potential problems which could arise if, for example, he was absent when Marlowe 'phoned. But luck was on his side. He had just walked into the hall off the last step of the stairs, when the telephone rang. As nobody was about, he let it ring for several seconds before picking up the receiver.

It was Marlowe again, and as he requested, Harry identified himself.

"Right, Guest. Are you listening carefully?"

"Yes, Mr. Marlowe."

"First we check our watches. I make it half past nine – a.m."

"Correct. My watch has that time."

"I will give you plenty of time. You are to await my call from the first kiosk outside St. Aubyn station at noon sharp. Twelve o'clock. Which gives you well over two hours."

233

Harry replied. "Twelve noon at the first telephone box outside St. Aubyn station, today."

Marlowe, as an added security measure, gave Harry the telephone number of the station box, which he jotted down in his diary.

"All this is a tight security procedure. Get it? Any questions, Guest?"

"No."

The 'phone was slammed in place with a harsh click which resounded in Harry's ear.

Harry's day was free. He had planned to go to the beach, but instead about eleven o'clock he drove over to St. Aubyn. Thinking it would be prudent, he put his car into the car park on the far side of the station. He was becoming very cautious as if he was being watched. After sitting for a few minutes, he left the car, locking it, and at a leisurely pace strolled to the station kiosks to wait for the noon-day call. He was a little worried in case he would find the telephone occupied, but it was free. Looking presently at his watch he saw the dial at twelve o'clock. Immediately the telephone began its regular ring-ring. Harry picked up the 'phone. "Guest, here."

The deep voice spoke. "Is that you, Guest?"

The unctuous and theatrical sound, reminiscent of Brucey's remembered voice, annoyed Harry so that he responded angrily.

"Yes, it is," he said. "And let's get one thing straight. I know who you are, Parkinson."

"Oh, 'Parkinson', is it? But, you just listen to me, Guest. You're in no position to be rash. Yes, so you've guessed correctly. I am Brucey's older brother, George. It changes nothing at all. So, here are your instructions."

Parkinson then gave simple directions, laced with a chilling warning.

234

"This is important. Don't try any funny stuff on me. Do not go to the police. Come alone and unarmed – that is if you wish Alex Penhalion to avoid my Brucey's fate."

He paused. Then gravely continued. "The 23rd September is, I expect you remember, the anniversary of Brucey's murder."

As Harry angrily denied this charge, Parkinson roared into the receiver, "Shut up, Guest, and remember Alex Penhalion."

After a pause he spoke in a quieter voice.

"Right, since I make myself clear, let me explain that I have chosen as our meeting place, on this special day, the very peak of Red Bluff point, because it is the place directly above the natural tomb where my brother lies unburied. Have you got that?"

"Yes."

Parkinson continued. "One more thing, you must approach the top of Red Bluff from the West side and you must arrive on time – neither early, nor late – at 5.30 on the 23rd. Half past five. It is unlikely that anybody else will be about at dusk, but if they are, we shall wait separately by the edge of the cliff until we are alone. Got it?"

"Yes."

"And the recognition code will be as follows: I shall say 'Marlowe' and you will reply 'Cellini'."

"Yes, understood."

"Then comes the hand-over. You will place the Cellini at your feet and step well back several paces. Yes?"

"Yes."

"Finally I shall put the diary and your copy letter on the ground and pick up the Cellini. Yes?"

As the voice ceased, Harry remained silent.

Impatiently Parkinson shouted, "Do you understand, Guest? You bring the Cellini."

When Harry said, "Yes", Parkinson repeated, "So, in three days time – on the 23rd September – five thirty – dusk

– at Red Bluff point – from the West – with the Cellini," and rang off without another word.

Harry drove back to the Red House, subdued and thoughtful. Of course George had arranged the meeting on the 23rd September, which he had guessed to be the anniversary of his brother's death, the date which he had seen entered in Brucey's diary. He was not to know of the incredible change of plans, which had brought the date of death to the 25th September instead.

In spite of being depressed, Harry was in fact experiencing an upsurge in his spirits. It was the same in war, when spirits rose once troops had received battle orders. A firm direction replaced dark forebodings. At last he knew where he was going.

II

It was the 23rd September, 1947. Alex was reading *The Daily Telegraph* and the date caught her eye. Oh, God, yes. The date of Harry's first attempt on the cave, a year ago. She laid the paper aside. Earlier on Harry had surprised her.

"Alex, I hope it's alright by you. But I want to get on with some more research at the Plymouth library. I'll make a day out of it and have a really good look round this time. See what more I can come up with on Marlowe. So, I'll be back a bit late."

She thought it was unlike him. Why hadn't he brought it up before, as he would normally have done? And why hadn't he mentioned wanting to do more research? He was tense. That was it. Something was wrong. Little things. He had changed lately. Had it all started with the unexpected phone call he received, when somebody wanted to send correspondence to the Red House? And she was puzzled - at any rate she was now she thought about it – that he had never confided in her about it. Why?

She could not help worrying. Eventually, however, towards the end of the day, she walked into the garden to think things over, and sat on a bench by the flower beds. Below her, against a steep bank, stood the old Victorian conservatory, where the gardener Fred, was talking to Molly, the daily help, preparing flowers together.

Closing her eyes she let her thoughts drift into a maze, at the same time absorbing the warm rays of the sun on her face. Peaceful. As her mind trailed, something struck her sharply into an alert state. She opened her eyes and blinked after the darkness of her rest. She was listening hard. It was a word she had overheard between Fred and Molly.

Molly emerged from the conservatory as she answered Fred's question. "It was in the afternoon. Mr. Guest brought it down from the attic."

"And you say it was an old brief-case?"

"That's it. A black one."

Alex asked herself, "Why on earth would Harry want the old brief case?" She was perplexed and cross. "Why hadn't he told me anyway?"

She had never panicked in her life, but she suddenly felt afraid; and for no apparent reason she knew she was on the verge of a panic attack.

She began to detail her worries, listing them in her head: the anniversary date of the cave deaths the day after tomorrow; Harry's sudden decision to leave for Plymouth all day; his casualness in failing to talk to her about something which she believed was worrying him; not telling her about the correspondent who wanted to write to him at the Red House; and now, not saying about the borrowed brief-case – a trivial matter if everything else was straightforward. But he was not behaving like his open self.

And, also, when he left her this morning, his last words were odd. "Don't answer any calls during the day, Alex."

"Why should there be a call?" she had asked.

With a smile he replied, "No reason. But, don't anyway." Until this moment she had suppressed his remarks from her mind.

Abruptly Alex came to a decision. She would go up to the attic – at once. She went upstairs, walking almost without thinking, as if her footsteps were leading her. When she reached the wide landing, she found she was trembling. She did not believe that Harry could deceive her, but she was frightened about what she would find. There was nobody about as she pulled down the folding steps from the trap door. Clambering into the attic, she crossed the long room and pushed a trunk under the niche where the casket lay. Climbing up she stretched her hand into the hiding place, but there was nothing there. She knew the Cellini had been removed before she raised her arm, but confirmation of her fears on finding the empty space was a harsh blow. She let herself fold slowly into a sitting position on the trunk, and then burst into tears.

Alex was not going to let herself be defeated. She told herself: Harry must have left something for me. He knew he couldn't do it openly. And he wouldn't let me down. But what would he do? Where was she to search for the answer and what was she looking for? She cast her eyes round the attic, but it was altogether too full for her to hope to find anything there. So, she said, "I'll try Harry's bedroom. It's the only place."

Closing the attic as she raised the steps, she made her way to the bedroom which Harry always occupied when he stayed. She searched everywhere in the room, even in the wardrobe. Harry had told her how he had pushed his Post Office book into a surface crack inside the cupboard, so as to conceal the Leander letter with the book. But there was nothing to be found in it. As she remembered last year's events, it came to her that Harry had put the Leander copy letter beneath his clean clothes in the chest of drawers, because it was an unlikely hiding place for anyone to search. Of course!

She jerked the drawers open. His clothes lay tidily side by side. And, when she lifted a green sweater from the bottom of the drawer, she found a letter consisting of several pages. Anxiously she sat on Harry's bed and read it.

She was horrified and yet fascinated at Marlowe's blackmail letter.

Then at the foot of the last page, Harry had written an additional note as follows:

"Alex. Marlowe is George Parkinson. I have agreed to meet him with the Cellini on Red Bluff at 5.30 p.m. this evening. If you find this, don't try to follow me. I shall see you later on to-night.

All my love, Harry – 23rd September, 1947."

Reading the last line, she thought, No wonder Harry had been upset. And he must have decided to shield me from all the worries over this bizarre affair by dealing with the situation on his own. But, why didn't he think of sharing it with me?

She stood up instantly, exclaiming aloud, "It's late. I must get there in time – and I know what I must do."

That evening Harry drove his car back from Plymouth and parked it out of sight under the trees in the woods beside the Lavington Road near the Western Cove 'bus stop. Locking the car he walked down the public footpath, crossed over the lane below the Red House and past the black-tarred store by the beach. He walked steadily up Red Bluff until he reached the summit, where he looked round at the magnificent view. Beyond the Bluff to the East lay the sea, reflecting a shimmering, red glow on its surface from the light of the dying sun. It felt exactly as if he was setting out on patrol in war-time, his senses keyed up, acutely aware of everything about him, alert to each detail impressed by the prick of danger ahead. As he stood breathing in the night air, he caught sight of a colourful fringe of flowers. A plant, which he could not remember noticing before had established itself there; clumps of pink thrift were growing on the ledge between the rock and the turf.

Glancing at his watch, he could see the face and time at twenty eight minutes past five. But there was no sign of anyone else on the headland. He peered through the fading light in all directions. And then the man was there. Less than a minute later, he saw Parkinson's outline against the skyline. First his head came into view, moving as he climbed the steep path, then his shoulders and at last he was stalking, long-legged, towards the top, dead on time. Harry shivered. The silhouette before him was a precise image of the dead Brucey, so like him was the older brother in the twilight. George Parkinson stopped not far from the edge at the very peak of Red Bluff.

Tense, the two stared at each other.

It was Parkinson who gruffly exclaimed the name, "Marlowe!"

Harry quietly replied, "Cellini."

Parkinson asked, "You have the Cellini with you?"

"Yes."

"As we agreed, now place the Cellini on the ground at your feet. Then take several paces back."

"And your part of the bargain?" Harry enquired.

"I shall exchange the diary and the copy letter, and then I shall leave. You will stay here until six o'clock before you go. Understand?"

"Yes."

Harry removed the casket from the old brief-case which he had found in the attic, and put it on the grass before him. Glaring, he took three steps back.

Parkinson immediately strode across and knelt beside the casket. Harry saw him drop, casually, what appeared to be a small object as he seized the casket with his left hand. Eagerly but clumsily, he wrenched open the casket. It was a dazzling moment there in the cool, evening air. As the lid fell back, a ray of red sunlight sparked a glint from the gleaming gold and silver surfaces within. Above the wind, Harry heard the tall man's sharp intake of breath.

Recalling the events later, Harry believed that nobody could have anticipated the speed of Parkinson's next, sudden and treacherous movement; fast as a flash of light on the sea, his right hand moved to his side and back again, bringing forward the squat shape of what looked like an American army pistol.

Slowly Parkinson stood up, pointing the pistol before him and at the same time jerking the weapon sideways, indicating that he wanted Harry to move nearer to the cliff edge.

In the clear night, listening to the sound of the wind on the Bluff and the constant breaking waves below, Harry stood quite still, his nerves at a pitch to detect any slight noise or change in his surroundings. It was a very faint sound, he was sure he had heard coming from behind Parkinson. Somebody was approaching from the East. Shortly after Harry could see a slight, dark shape walking towards him and he thought he could just detect the soft scrape of light footsteps. He wondered how Parkinson could fail to remain unaware of the movements.

Parkinson however was concerned exclusively with Harry. He made another, angry gesture, twisting his right wrist, and using the pistol as a pointer. He was still trying to get Harry to move dangerously near to the precipice. At the same time he gave a parade-ground command. "Move."

Harry stepped sideways, but, as he also saw the unknown walker closing in, he shouted, "Look out – behind you!"

The tall, sepulchral Parkinson, standing gaunt and thin in the night, remained upright. "What absurdity is this? The oldest ploy in the game?" he asked.

But Harry repeated his shouted warning, more urgently now. "Look out – just behind you!"

Simultaneously Parkinson realised that there really was somebody behind him, for as if he too had heard something, he glanced quickly over his shoulder.

It was as though Harry had slipped back in time and had returned to the cave, far beneath his feet, where nearly a year ago he had tackled the younger brother. Seeing that Parkinson was off his guard, Harry acted. Careless of life, trapped with no alternative, he flung himself across the gap between them. The force of his heavy frame as he fell against Parkinson's legs, sent the man rolling to the ground. The casket was instantly jolted out of his hand. It tumbled away from him, turning over and over towards the end of the Bluff, until slowing down, it teetered there before plunging out of sight into the sea.

The heavy fall had also dislodged the pistol from Parkinson's hand, and the weapon slipped over the grass after the casket, but came to rest near the edge. Harry launched himself from the grass in the direction of the pistol. To the unknown watcher behind them, it must have looked like some crazy game of cricket, where two fielders both dived in a desperate effort to catch a ball, hit to the boundary lip of Red Bluff by the vigorous stroke of an unseen batsman. Instinctively Parkinson likewise threw himself in a fury towards the spot where the pistol nestled in the grass. But, Harry was there first and, grabbing the pistol, he snatched it to his chest, as Parkinson struck the ground nearby. Slithering so fast, at full stretch over the smoothly flattened grass, he could not stop himself. Frantically he tried to grasp Harry by the coat as he passed, but he missed and swung sideways towards the edge of the cliff. At the last moment he managed to check his speed by clinging to the long grass with both hands and hooking one foot precariously in a rocky cleft. But his body's momentum was too great for him to keep his hold. He called out pitifully, "Help me! Help me!"

Then, suddenly he was gone with a terrible scream. The words, "Help me!" rapidly receded as he dropped from the heights to the sea and the rocks below.

Harry lay still, before easing himself upright and going over to peer down. It was too dark to make out more than the white strips of breaking waves on the black rocks. There was no sign of Parkinson.

When he turned, he saw Alex. She was staring at the edge, appalled at what she had witnessed, hardly believing that it had actually happened.

For a long while they looked into each others' eyes, standing still, staring, barely comprehending the enormity of what they had both experienced. When eventually they stirred, they moved as one, quickly coming together. In this way they held each other closely, Alex's head against Harry's shoulder as he gazed unseeing into the gathering darkness. It seemed an age before they separated.

But Alex pulled Harry to her again. She began to whisper in his ear. Slowly, out of the shock of the events, they spoke quietly, close to each other, going over the wretched details of the past dreadful days, each gradually telling the other everything they knew. But in the end the stark facts remained. As a result of the search for Cellini's crucifix, three men and one woman had died and the casket, with its priceless treasure, now lay on the sea-bed.

Presently the two fell silent. Harry bent down and picked up the pistol. As he examined it, he heard Alex call out, "What's this?"

She was picking up something from the grass and he guessed that she was holding the diary which Parkinson must have discarded. She passed it to him. In the remaining half-light, he flicked over the diary's pages, noting that it covered the year 1946. It was filled with regular and detailed entries, finishing however before the end of September, the last entry was: "To-morrow. Meet Leander in Cornwall to follow Guest to Red Bluff cave and the Cellini."

Harry also unfolded a crumpled paper which had been clipped to the back of the diary. He recognised his own handwriting. It was his copied version of ancestor Leander's letter to his father.

Without saying a word Harry tucked the diary and letter together into his top jacket pocket. Then he removed the ammunition clip from its slot in the base of the pistol butt, and, as if he was playing ducks-and-drakes, cast the magazine, loaded with bullets, out into the sea. Next, he took from his pocket the diary with the letter, folding them length-ways. Then he forced them inside the empty pistol butt.

Pausing to look at Alex, he threw the pistol violently into the night, where arcing high, it disappeared to join the clip already at the bottom of the sea. Now the diary could not accidentally fall, or by a strange chance be carried by the wind to some landing place where it might be recovered. The sea would soon dissolve the inked records for all time.

As he was about to leave, he saw the black brief-case lying empty, where he had cast it. Snatching it up nervously, he stared about him, but nothing else had been left.

The wind plucked at Alex's hair and the darkness closed in on them. Holding each other tightly, they walked away from the brink.

Epilogue

If in the following year, 1948, Harry Guest had instructed experts to authenticate the Leander Penhalion letter of 30th Jun, 1593, they would have had no difficulty in certifying that the letter was genuine, written at the end of the sixteenth century. But they would have been unable to corroborate the details of the extraordinary tale about the arrest of Christopher Marlowe on a charge of forgery in January, 1592, as Leander had described in the letter to his father. In fact historical confirmation of the playwright's involvement in the passing of forged coins was not established until Prof. Robert E. Wernham discovered the evidence in 1976, that Sir Robert Sidney, brother of Sir Philip Sydney, took Marlowe as a prisoner together with a goldsmith in Flushing in 1593. The prisoners, who were charged with attempted coining, admitted the charge but argued that only one Dutch shilling made of "plain pewter and with half an eye to be discovered" had been passed. Subsequently they were deported to England, where they were eventually freed.

"My gold, my gold, and all my wealth is gone!"
– The Jew of Malta – Christopher Marlowe

ISBN 142510990-X